ONE WILL TOO MANY

A JULIA FAIRCHILD MYSTERY

PJ PETERSON

Debbie —
Enjoy!
PJ Peterson

FINNGIRL, LLC

For More Information contact

pj@pjpetersonauthor.com

ISBN paperback 978-1-7335674-8-9

www.pjpetersonauthor.com

Finngirl, LLC

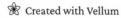 Created with Vellum

This book is dedicated to those who fight for justice.

CHAPTER 1

THE LITTLE THEATRE

J ulia frowned at her beeper as she pulled into the physicians' parking lot at the hospital. It had already gone off three times since her call day had started barely thirty minutes before, at seven a.m. She hoped it wasn't a harbinger of the weekend ahead of her. She sighed a breath of relief when she saw that the latest page was a message to call her friend Pam, rather than the more typical request to call the hospital's emergency department. But why would she be calling so early on a Saturday morning?

After taking care of important email messages, checking the hospital computer for overnight admissions and printing the list of patients to see on morning rounds, Julia checked in with the unit secretary in the intensive care unit.

"Good morning, Jeanne. How's Mrs. Benson doing today?"

Jeanne looked up from the monitor screen with its list of current patients. "Oh, hi, Dr. Fairchild. I hear she's doing well. How's call going so far?"

"Just great, but it's early." Julia crossed her fingers and

rapped her knuckles on the wooden frame of the nurses' station, just in case.

"I hope it stays that way for you. Let me get Mrs. Benson's nurse for you. I overhead Larry tell the other nurse she's probably ready to transfer to the step-down unit." Jeanne walked to one of the private rooms and knocked lightly on the glass door as she slid it open. "Larry, Dr. Fairchild is here to see Mrs. Benson."

A moment later, Larry, one of the specialized nurses working the twelve-hour day shift, briefed Julia on her patient's status—vital signs were stable, no chest pain during the night, no rhythm abnormalities—as they walked into the room.

"Good morning, Mrs. Benson," said Julia. "Your nurse tells me that you are doing very well today. How are you feeling?"

"Dr. Fairchild, I feel so much better today. My breathing is easier and I even slept a few hours. Do you know how bad my heart attack was? Is my heart going to be okay? Am I going to be able to go to San Francisco for Thanksgiving to see my son and his family?" She stopped talking to take a breath and a sip of water.

"Whoa! You are clearly more energetic today," Julia said as she logged onto the bedside computer. "Let's see what the tests say." Julia scrolled through the screens showing the studies that had been done on Mrs. Benson. "The heart damage looks mild on the echocardiogram. The cardiologist's note says you don't need any more testing right now unless you have more pain." Julia put her stethoscope in her ears. "If your heart sounds strong and your lungs are as clear as your nurse Larry said they were, I'll transfer you to the cardiology floor."

Mrs. Benson sat up straight and crossed her fingers while Julia listened carefully.

"Sounds good," Julia announced, placing her stethoscope around her neck. "One more day in the hospital, then you should be able to go home tomorrow."

"I would be a little afraid to go home alone today, but I'm sure I'll feel well enough tomorrow. Now, what about Thanksgiving in San Francisco?"

"Right now that's a maybe," said Julia. "We'll discuss it again in a couple of weeks when I see you in the office." She wrote a brief note and the transfer orders in the electronic record before leaving the ICU to visit patients on other floors.

Julia dialed Pam's number while she walked the short distance to the cardiology unit where three of her patients waited to be seen.

Pam answered with audible wheezing.

"I got your message," said Julia. "What's going on? Is your asthma acting up again?"

"Not any worse than usual on a cold morning. But that's not why I called."

"Okay, so what *is* going on?"

"I was worried you wouldn't be able to call right back. The answering service said you were on call, and I know it can get crazy busy. Anyway, my sister Susie called me from Seattle. She's visiting Mom and said she fell and broke her hip while Susie was outside doing a bit of yardwork. Now she's beside herself and needs me to come up and help her manage Mom. You know how confused she gets sometimes. Mom, I mean, not Susie." Pam paused for a moment and Julia heard the whoosh of her inhaler.

"Okay. Do you need me to feed your dog or something while you're gone?" Julia had watched Pam's Shetland collie at other times when her friend had to be out of town for a few days.

"Thanks, but not that. I'm going to take Princess with me. I need something even more important than that."

"Pam, since when is anything more important than your dog?" Julia chuckled.

Pam laughed. "Well, nothing is, really, but I do have a huge favor to ask. I promised Drake I would go with him to that theatre fundraiser tonight. And now I can't go. He's the master of ceremonies and needs someone to help work the crowd and talk up the need for refurbishing the building. The theatre restoration committee has a goal of raising two million dollars and this is the kickoff event. Could you go in my place? Please?"

Well, that was awkward! Julia would do anything to help Pam, but what would Alex think of her going with someone else? Julia and Alex had been dating for a few months, and he was on the board of directors for the theatre so had already invited her himself. And she'd declined.

"Do you remember that I wasn't going to go with Alex because I'm on call and never know when I am going to be called away to the ICU or the emergency department? So Alex is going alone. Isn't there someone else who could take your place as Drake's date tonight? What about your friend, Lexie?"

"I understand about you and Alex. I talked with Drake and he called Alex and Alex said he's okay with you going with Drake this time. You would only need to stay a couple of hours. Please, Julia. Drake really needs you. *I* need you." Her voice trembled.

Julia considered the request for a moment before replying. "Okay, Pam. I'll do it. I'm in support of the project anyway. I suppose I have to go fancy."

"Julia, thanks! Yes, it's fancy. Wear one of those gorgeous outfits that you always find for the hospital's holiday gala. You'll look perfect. Drake said he could pick you up at six thirty. Now I've gotta get on the road to Mom's house before

Susie commits hara-kiri. I'll call you tomorrow to see how it went." And she was gone.

Julia stared at the silent phone, smiling, and shook her head as she finally replaced the receiver in the cradle at the nurses' station. She never knew what kind of predicament Pam was going to get her into next. At least she liked Drake well enough, and she enjoyed dressing up now and then. She hoped the beeper would be quiet for the event, or maybe she could sweet-talk one of her partners into covering calls for a couple of hours.

It was early afternoon before Julia finished seeing all the patients. She signed charts in medical records, read electrocardiograms in the cardiology unit, and reviewed lab and x-ray reports of the inpatients before heading home to eat a quick lunch and toss laundry into the washing machine.

Her home office answering machine was beeping and flashing the number "3" as she entered. The first message was from Pam, informing her that she would try paging her. The second one was a hang-up. A robocall, probably. The third caller was Alex, asking her to call him when she got home.

She thought back to Pam's call earlier. Pam was her closest friend, though they hadn't known each other until they met at a chamber of commerce "After Hours" event three years earlier that had been hosted by her hospital, St. Jerome Medical Center. Julia had attended only because her boss, the vice president for the medical group, had asked her to be present as one of the leaders within the organization. She and Pam had hit it off during their chat as they discovered several common interests.

Pam Stewart was the human resources vice president at ESCO, Emerson Sons and Company—the local pulp and paper mill. She had grown up in Parkview, gone to the bigger of the two high schools in town, and pledged to Kappa Kappa Gamma at the University of Washington. The sorority pledging had thrilled her mom, but not Pam. She eventually moved into the dorms instead. She graduated with degrees in business and psychology. Despite her stated plan to live and work in a big city when she was a grown-up, she was lured back to her hometown by the area's largest employer and seemed content.

Pam was fun to be around and liked to do many of the same things that Julia enjoyed. She was tall and lithe, blonde, a little kooky, and single. Having grown up in Parkview, she had a ton of local knowledge and seemed to know something about practically every person in the town of about 38,000. Her mom had been widowed at a young age and remarried an older man from Seattle. After he died she stayed there, having developed a network of friends, in addition to the convenience of having Pam's older sister Susie living close by.

Julia had followed a similar course. She had grown up with five brothers and sisters on a small farm ten miles down the highway. At the age of seven she knew she wanted to be a doctor so she could help people. At 5 foot 6 inches with a mop of brown hair, sparkly blue eyes and high cheekbones, she looked every bit like her Finnish ancestors. She was blessed (cursed?) with a stubborn streak that the Finns call *sisu*. She'd had to overcome her parents' arguments that she didn't know what she was getting into and that she would find it hard to have a family *and* be a doctor. She went to medical school anyway and completed a challenging internal medicine residency. She had planned to do a fellowship in gastroenterology, but her grandma became ill and pleaded with her to come back to Parkview. "You'll like it," she had said in her Finn-glish accent. Julia promised to try it for six months, although her grandma died before she was able to see Julia keep her promise.

Five years later she was glad she had landed in her home area and frequently told her patients that she was still on her six-month trial. Julia figured that her grandma was smiling down on her from Heaven, pleased with her decision. Grandma had been correct that Julia would end up enjoying her practice of medicine in Parkview. Every now and then Julia felt wistful and wondered what it would have been like to be a doctor in a big city, but she knew she would miss the patients who had become like part of her family. The only thing missing in her life was starting her own family. She only hoped her parents' argument about the difficulty of blending being a doctor and having a family would turn out wrong. Alex, at least so far, had seemed to accept her crazy schedule as a doctor. She sighed and called Alex after checking on her laundry.

"Hello, Julia. Knight in shining armor at your service," Alex said glibly.

Julia laughed. "Sounds interesting. Do I have the wrong number?"

"I hope not. I couldn't say that to just anyone who calls."

"I hope not! What's up?"

"I just wanted to check with you on this shindig tonight. I'm planning to go even though I'd rather not. It's hard to get out of it with me being on the board of directors. I hope you don't mind that I told Drake you could sub for Pam even though you bailed on me."

She cringed at the word bailed. The last thing she wanted was to jeopardize their relationship. "I hope that Drake and Pam didn't pressure you to be okay with that. You know I would have loved to go with you, and the only reason I declined," she strategically used declined versus bailed, "was because I'm on call. Remember?"

"I know, and your presence will be an asset. If you get called away, it will only reinforce your dedication to your profession. And so be it. Anything you can do to promote the need for renovating the little theatre at the gala will help to get some of these people to open their wallets. People do think a lot of you, you know." He laid out his case as if he were talking to a jury at the end of a trial.

"But will people think I ditched you if I show up with Drake? I wouldn't want people to talk."

"No problem. I'll make it clear that we are still an item, and that you are there on behalf of those supporting the cause."

"Hm. You are so noble and kind. And you know I'm a sucker for that kind of flattery. As for being on call, Jason agreed to cover me for a few hours. I can return the favor some other weekend."

"That's great. I'm looking forward to seeing you and counting the money at the end of the evening. By the way, Drake said to tell you that he'll have to meet you there instead. He forgot that he had to do something so he can't pick you up. Shall I give you a ride?"

"Thanks for the offer, but no. I'll want to have my own car in case I really do have to leave early. I'll see you there. Is six thirty okay?"

"That would be good. Definitely no later than that. It'll give you some time to chat up a few folks and loosen some pocket-books before dinner starts at eight o'clock. Looking forward to seeing you, Beautiful."

"Same here. Bye."

Alex Gibson was an attorney, a transplant from the big city of Hartford, where he had grown tired of the corporate world. He'd told Julia he had found his way to Parkview several years earlier through a friend's recommendation and loved the small town with its quirks, interesting people, and plenty of general legal work to keep him busy. Julia had met him three months earlier at a benefit for the local homeless shelter. They had been dating pretty much steadily since that time.

He was involved in several community humanitarian organizations in addition to the project to restore the city's original performing arts theatre. Julia had been attracted to his kind heart and integrity in addition to his chiseled good looks with a cleft chin. Thick sandy blond hair with a touch of gray and dark blue-gray eyes didn't hurt either. Most importantly, as an attorney he, too, occasionally found that his career impacted his private plans. This made him more comfortable with the fact that she was a physician and dedicated to her craft. She couldn't say that about all men. That kind of guy was indeed rare in a smaller community like Parkview.

While Julia liked spending time with Alex, she was still gun-shy after her Paris rendezvous with an earlier beau, Josh Larson. She had fantasized a romantic vacation seeing Paris as his guest the previous spring, but it was not to be. The death of his partner early in her visit, with Josh having been considered a prime suspect, put a major damper on the fun. To top it off he had admitted on the last day of her visit that he had started seeing someone else. Julia had been crushed. It reinforced her worry that she would never meet the right man who loved and appreciated her and could manage the crazy personal life of a dedicated physician. Her relationship with Alex was in the very early stages but she gave herself permission to be optimistic that it might develop into something special. And long-lasting.

Julia glared at her pager when it beeped, breaking her reverie. The medical floor needed her, fortunately, instead of the emergency department. After taking care of the orders for a patient who needed intravenous medication, she searched her closet for the right attire for the evening. She settled on a shimmery, charcoal-gray, floor-length skirt paired with a three-quarter-sleeved, black velvet top with a deep V-neck and wide, black satin collar. She would add a bold, silver pendant and small diamond earrings to complete the sophisticated ensemble.

JULIA ARRIVED at the Hotel Montpelier just as Drake drove up. She took advantage of his simultaneous presence to make a proper entrance to the celebration in the Hotel's grand ballroom. It had recently been refurbished to its original grandeur from the early 1920s. She admired the beauty of the ceilings with their art deco design, recently uncovered by the removal of a false ceiling from a previous upgrade. The beautiful wood floor with exquisite inlaid mosaics shone from a recent floor polishing. The cherry and mahogany woodwork glistened in the light from the elegant crystal chandeliers which had also been hidden until now.

Julia and Drake were greeted by some of the other members of the restoration committee. Drake was the designated master of ceremonies while Julia's primary duty was to personally welcome as many of the potential donors as possible and say a few words in support of the project. He certainly looked the part tonight in a well-cut, black velvet tuxedo. His dark hair was touched with silver—just enough to give him a classy look. He stood tall and proud as he walked through the crowd, nodding to some and saying a word or two to other attendees.

Julia searched the assembled festival attendees for familiar faces as Drake gently guided her to an older man and woman. He placed his hand at the small of her back as he addressed the wealthy couple. "Julia, I'd like to introduce Mr. and Mrs.

George Oglethorpe. They have been longtime supporters of the theatre."

Julia stepped forward a half-step and extended her hand. "I'm Julia Fairchild. I'm honored to meet you. I love our theatre, too."

The woman's face brightened as she recognized the name. "Of course! *Dr.* Fairchild. Call me Anna. I've heard a lot of good things about you." She took Julia's hand in both of hers. "You're so young and pretty for a doctor."

Julia reddened. She felt a little mousey most days, but conceded to herself that she did clean up nicely for such events. "Thank you. I was blessed with good genes. How long have you and your husband lived in Parkview?"

"My goodness. Forever. Right out of college, anyway. George heard about the paper mill here looking for mechanical engineers and applied right away." She smiled proudly at him. "We love the town and were never inclined to leave once we settled in. Isn't that right, dear?" Her husband nodded between sips of his drink. "Are you from here?"

"Not from Parkview. I was raised on a small farm fifteen miles down the highway. My grandma persuaded me to come home and here I am." Julia felt her eyes well up as she recalled warm memories of time spent with her grandparents. "Thank you for your support of our lovely theatre. The restoration committee will be sharing the plans for the renovation during the program."

Julia felt Drake's arm around her waist as he interceded. "Thank you for coming this evening. Please excuse us. I see someone who is clamoring to talk with Dr. Fairchild before the dinner starts."

Drake took Julia's arm and as they turned around they almost bumped into Gregory Lantz and his wife, Sandy, who had been standing right behind them. "Greg! So good to see you here tonight. Thanks for coming." They exchanged nods and handshakes. "Julia is standing in for Karen tonight. She's also supporting the project." Julia smiled and nodded. Aside from the perfunctory smiles Julia sensed a tension between the men, and she moved a step away from Drake to better observe them both.

Greg stirred his gin and tonic vigorously. "I've talked with some of the members of the board at the bank, but I don't have a definite commitment yet for a donation. I think we can come through for fifty thousand dollars. But nothing close to the million dollars that everyone seems to think the bank can donate."

"Greg, any amount would be great. I understand it's been a little tough with the new bank still getting started." Drake Ashford was the president of the older, long-established Parkview National Bank. He was aware that despite heavy advertising and promotions, the new River City Community Bank was not yet meeting expectations. He was also acutely sensitive to the loss of some of his own banking clients to the new bank, where Greg was vice president.

Greg bristled. "Actually, we're meeting our numbers and seeing new business every day. I'd think you would have noticed already." He smirked.

"We've noticed a little change, but we're prepared to handle it." Drake took a large swallow of his scotch. "Please excuse us. I have some other people to greet. Talk to you later, Greg." Drake and Julia moved away.

"That man really annoys me," Drake said under his breath. "He's so naive. He doesn't see how Jay is using him. He's just a yes man. But I guess it makes him feel important."

"What do you mean?" Julia asked, nodding and smiling at some of the faces she recognized. She knew he referred to Jay Morrison, recently divorced and head of the new bank. She felt

Drake's hand shaking as he maneuvered her through the crowd.

"I'll tell you later. Too many ears here." He surveyed the guests nearby. "Let's see...there's Warren Pontell and his lovely wife, Sarah. He's talked about making a major contribution. His wife was a theatre actress in her younger days. And they have money to burn." He turned to Julia and wiggled his eyebrows, à la Groucho Marx.

Drake and Julia chatted with the Pontells for a few minutes, using the time to emphasize the benefits of the smaller venue of the little theatre. It was designed to be an intimate stage setting with seating for about 150 people. Until recently the area had been used for storage and was marginally functional for stage events in its current state.

Julia had found herself daydreaming but tuned back in when she heard Mr. Pontell say, "We'd like to donate fifty thousand dollars for the little theatre. Perhaps you can find a way to let us have something to say about naming it." He grinned broadly as his wife beamed.

"Warren, that's wonderful!" said Drake. "I'll talk with the board of directors about naming opportunities. Let me get back to you on details for your donation. Thank you."

Now grinning, Drake gently guided Julia toward Adam Johns, an influential man in the local union hierarchy, and his wife. He had started working at ESCO Paper Company right out of high school and had worked his way up from the labor pool to an electrician apprenticeship and then to a journeyman electrician. His constituents considered him to be fair and honest. He had an unofficial status in the union as a leader, although he didn't have an elected or paid position as such.

Adam tugged at the neck of his dress shirt and pulled at the bottom of his dark blue waistcoat. The jacket gaped over his generous girth. He looked uncomfortable in his tuxedo. Julia was sure her mother would have said something like "putting perfume on a goat," but most likely his wife had insisted he dress up for this occasion. He certainly looked impressive at his height of six foot three.

"Mr. and Mrs. Johns, good evening," said Drake as he offered his hand. "Do you know Dr. Julia Fairchild? She's helping to support the theatre restoration project, as we all are."

"We sure do," said Adam, returning the handshake. "Dr. Fairchild, you took care of my mom several years back. She was pretty sick but you got her well and she's fine now. Thanks to you. In fact, she's going on a cruise through the Panama Canal with her church group this coming week. She's always wanted to go on that trip."

"You're welcome, Mr. Johns. I do remember your mom— Violette, I believe? She's a lovely lady with a lot of spunk." Julia shook his hand before turning to his wife. "Pleased to meet you, Mrs. Johns."

Mr. Johns turned back to Drake. "Mr. Ashford, some of the guys at the mill want to know if you had talked with our union officials yet about the stock trading going on with our pension funds. And if you know anything, they hope you can tell them. And call me Adam. My wife is Linda."

"Yes, Adam. I talked with a Scott Sowders in Portland. He's looking into whether those trading fees can be traced back to any individuals. May I call you when I know something more?"

"Sure. You can call me at ESCO. The operator knows how to reach me. Thanks a lot, Mr. Ashford."

"You can call me Drake, please. I'll call you soon and we'll go from there. Thanks again for being here tonight."

"Hey. It's an alright party. My wife is always trying to get me to gussy up. It's more fun than I thought it would be." He grinned and saluted with his cocktail.

Julia saw the auctioneer heading their way and alerted Drake. "I'll check my lipstick while you talk with him. Where are we sitting?"

"Main table," he said, pointing to the center of the long side of the room. He scowled. "Unfortunately, it appears we're seated next to Jay Morrison, of all people."

CHAPTER 2

GOING, GOING, GONE

J ulia's first impression of the newly renovated ladies' room was that it resembled an Italian boudoir, although she'd never been in one. The ornate, gold-flocked wallpaper, grainy black granite vanity top, and red-trimmed mirrors looked like something imported from the Roaring Twenties, the era when the hotel had been built.

She was adjusting her skirt in preparation to step out of the stall when she heard two voices arguing as they entered the room. A glass clinked on the vanity, followed by the sound of water running in the sink as she waited.

"It's not Jay's fault that Greg is in the middle of the mess. He shouldn't have stuck his nose in it," said the first angry voice. "Darn. I'll have to take this dress to the dry cleaners to get the rest of the wine out."

"Jay gave him the assignment. How could Greg refuse? Jay *is* his boss, you know," replied the second voice, slurring some of her words.

"Well," said the first voice, "Greg went too far." Paper towels crinkled.

"And how would he have known that?"

"It doesn't take a rocket scientist to figure out what offshore banks are for," said the first voice with an edge of impatience.

"But he didn't know that's what it was!"

"He should have. He's a banker, for Pete's sake," said the first voice more angrily. The lid of the trash can clanged shut.

The voices moved away then disappeared when the door opened and closed again. Julia recognized the first voice as Becca Morrison, Jay's ex-wife, and surmised that the second voice belonged to Sandy, Greg's wife. But what was it all about? She waited another moment to be sure they had moved away from the room's entrance. They hadn't been aware of her overhearing the conversation and she wanted to keep it that way.

Reentering the ballroom, Julia acknowledged several other guests, already seated and beginning on their main course, as she made her way to the head table. She skirted by a server who had just left a sumptuous-looking plate of petite beef tenderloins, sculpted mashed potatoes and grilled, buttery, fresh asparagus spears at her place. She took her seat next to Jay Morrison, the only son of wealthy parents, both of whom had died a few years back and left him very well off. He had been living on the East Coast for at least ten years before moving to Parkview about five years ago. He and a group of investors opened a new bank, River City Community Bank. There had been rumbles in the community about it at the time, with many expressing an opinion that the city hadn't needed another one.

She was surprised at the seating arrangement which placed Jay and Drake virtually next to each other, albeit she was seated between them. Julia decided to do her best to solicit a donation from Jay before Drake joined them.

"How nice to see you, Jay. I hear the new bank is doing well," said Julia, offering her hand.

"Thank you. The numbers are ahead of projections and the board of directors is pleased to be where we are at this stage of the game." Jay beamed his too-perfect-teeth smile at Julia. "Where's Alex tonight?"

Julia noticed that he was slurring his words. She pointed across the dance floor. "He's over there. That empty chair next to him is supposed to be mine. Yum. These beef tenderloins are delicious."

"Then why are you here?" He signaled to the waiter for another scotch, neat. "Did you break up or something?"

"No. We're fine. I'm playing at being Pam, Drake's flame, but only for the sake of the gala. She had to go out of town for a family emergency and begged me to take her place. With Alex's knowledge of course."

Jay relaxed his shoulders. "I'm glad to hear that—that you've not split up, I mean. By the way, do you know Sophia Alder?" He turned to the lovely young woman on his left. "Sophia, I'd like to introduce you to Dr. Julia Fairchild, one of our excellent physicians. Julia, meet Sophia."

The two women smiled at each other. "Sophia has done theatre work in San Francisco. And she's hoping to break into the movies."

Julia nodded at Sophia and smiled at the young server who was placing a dessert at each place. The cheesecake with blueberry sauce looked delicious.

"Parkview seems to be a quiet little town," said Sophia, "compared to San Francisco, that is. What do people even do around here?" She waved a hand in the air as if she had noticed a fly bothering her.

Julia flashed her best "I-know-your-kind-and-you-don't-fool-me" smile before launching into part of her spiel. "The quality and variety of entertainment here is improving all the time. Refurbishing the Parkview Theatre for Performing Arts will allow for expansion of what it can offer to the public, from children to adults. Generations of parents have watched their darlings in tap and ballet recitals on our stage. Even the—"

Drake's booming voice interrupted her, preventing further conversation. "Welcome, ladies and gentlemen, to the inaugural Theatre Grande Festival. The committee members hope you are enjoying the beauty of the hotel ballroom, the company of the other guests, and the excellent dinner service."

He paused for the polite applause. "As you know, this is the first major fundraiser for the Parkview Performing Arts theatre restoration project. The theatre's board of directors has wonderful plans for renovation of the little theatre in addition to improving the lobby, replacing the original 1925 seating, and upgrading the marquee." More applause.

"Joining us tonight is Bradley Taylor, our project consultant, who will explain this better than I can." Drake turned to Bradley, who was seated to his right. "It's all yours."

Julia glanced around the room as the consultant explained the project including the timeline and estimated costs. She saw that Greg and his wife, Sandy, sat at a table near the stage. He was a soft-looking, unpolished kind of guy. That was a contrast to Jay's perfect, expensive facade including his Armani suits. Sandy, who taught third grade at one of the town's elementary schools, wore a simple, taupe brocade cocktail dress, several seasons out of style.

Two tables over she spotted Becca Morrison, Jay's ex-wife, who appeared to be without a date for the evening. Their divorce had been less than amicable. Details had been splashed all over the local newspaper and rumors bubbled up in lunch conversations. Becca was a pretty woman with gorgeous, long chestnut hair, but her personality had a hard edge. She had told Julia that she inherited her hair from her Irish mother and the personality from her blackjack father. She wore a stunning long, off-the-shoulder, form-fitting dress in deep red. It surely hadn't come from any store in Parkview.

Once the live auction got underway and while the guests ate dessert and drank more wine, the bidding for progressive dinners, weekends at someone's beach house, and discounted cruises became intense. The professional auctioneer from Seattle knew how to tease money out of wallets with his gentle bantering and coaxing. Julia bid successfully on a pair of tickets for a ballet performance, dinner, and an overnight stay in one of the finer hotels in Portland. She was confident she could find a date when the time came. Even if Alex couldn't join her, her younger sister Carly was usually good for an event in a pinch. They had traveled together several times over the years and spent an occasional girls-only weekend at Carly's beach house.

Julia's beeper stayed quiet until 10:10 at which time it vibrated silently on the table. The phone number for the hospital's emergency department flashed on the screen. Her partner had said he'd cover her calls until ten o'clock. She hoped he'd had a quiet evening. Drake nodded when she tapped his shoulder and pointed to her pager, then headed to the foyer where she could make the call.

"Emergency department. Ginger speaking."

"Hi, Ginger. Dr. Fairchild here. What do you guys have for me?"

"Thanks for calling back so quickly. Dr. Gorman wants to talk with you. Hang on."

Julia listened as Dr. Gorman related the pertinent details of the elderly man who had presented with chest pain and was clinically stable but needed admission to the cardiology telemetry unit for overnight monitoring. She was grateful that he was willing to write the orders necessary until Julia made morning rounds. It wasn't required of the emergency department physicians but it saved her from having to make a midnight run to the hospital. "Thanks so much, Paul. I'll see him bright and early tomorrow."

Returning to her table, she noticed Jay noisily responding to something his date, Sophia, had said. He bobbed and weaved in his chair and slurred his words as he said, "I'm perfectly okay to drive you home. I've only had two little drinks."

"More like six, Jay," said Sophia, whispering loudly. "I'm not letting you drive. Hand me the keys." She held out a hand, the other hand on her hip.

"Nope. I'm driving. You can go home with someone else if you want." He crossed his arms and sulked.

Sophia glared at him. "I'll do just that. Now be quiet. The auction isn't quite finished yet."

Julia leaned back and whispered to Sophia behind Jay's back. "I'm leaving in about fifteen minutes. Morning rounds come early after a late evening. Can I drive you home?"

"Thanks. I'd appreciate that," said Sophia. "I have a room at the Grecian Inn. Is that out of your way?"

"Not at all. Once the bidding is done I need to talk with my friend Alex over there." She gestured across the room. "Then we can leave." Julia finished her glass of wine as the last item went up for bid. Several active bidders had pushed the cost for a beautiful sapphire and diamond ring donated by a generous local jeweler to more than four thousand dollars.

"Going once," said the auctioneer. He looked at Layton Andrews, a local attorney, one of the bidders. "Are you going to let that other guy buy that gorgeous ring for his wife?"

Layton smiled and said, "Yep."

"Going twice! Are you sure you don't want to buy this fine

piece of jewelry for the lovely woman sitting next to you?" he asked George Thomas, a dentist who raised an eyebrow and nodded without looking at his wife. She was wearing a modest diamond necklace and matching earrings which sparkled in the light.

"Gone! Sold to bidder number 143 for four thousand two hundred dollars!" Mark Shelton, orthopedic surgeon, grinned broadly and held up his wife's hand as he showed his bid card to the scouter. "Thank you, sir." The auctioneer wiped his glistening brow with a handkerchief. "Thanks to everyone tonight for supporting this worthy cause."

Drake stepped up to take the mike and waited for the applause to subside. "Thank you all for coming out tonight and for loving our historic theatre." He paused as Alex walked up to the podium and handed him an index card. Drake nodded at Alex, smiled broadly, and slowly scanned the audience. "You're going to love this number. The unofficial total for tonight's auction is two hundred fifty-two thousand one hundred dollars."

He waited for the exuberant round of applause. "There are a few of you who have indicated your intention to contribute for the project at a later date. One of us will be in touch. I promise." A soft titter rippled through the crowd. "Seriously, you can contact any of the members of the board, all of whom are listed on the program, or me. Our executive director, Marco Gianelli, is always happy to talk about money as well. Marco, will you stand, please?"

Marco stood and mimed a hats off, then applauded the audience.

"Now, as master of ceremonies, I declare the festival officially ended. Thank you, and drive home safely." Drake made a dramatic bow and saluted the guests.

Julia said a word of congratulations to Drake as he hugged

her gently and thanked her for her participation. She met Alex halfway across the room as he came toward her table. "What a lovely evening." She kissed him on the cheek as he took her hands.

"Dinner tomorrow night?"

Julia smiled, her dimples deep in her cheeks, blue eyes twinkling. "I'd love it. Thank you. I'm taking Sophia to her hotel, then heading home."

Alex scrunched his eyebrows. "Is there something wrong with Jay?"

"He's drunk and won't let Sophia drive," Julia explained. "Too macho for his own good, I suppose."

"Do you have to go to the hospital as well?"

"Thankfully, no. There was only one admission this evening and the emergency physician wrote holding orders until I can see the patient in the morning. I'll call you after I finish rounds. Okay?"

"Sure. I hope things stay quiet for the rest of the night," said Alex, kissing the tips of her fingers.

Julia found Sophia waiting in the lobby, checking her phone for email and messages, Julia presumed.

"Thanks so much for driving me home," said Sophia. "I get so irritated when Jay drinks as much as he did tonight. His driving scares me. His judgment goes out the window when he's drunk. And I feel a little queasy after that dinner so I didn't want to have to wait for him to be done."

"I'm glad to help. He seemed quarrelsome. Does he get drunk like this often?" Julia led the way across the entrance drive in front of the hotel. "My car is parked in the second row. It's the white coupe."

"Often enough. I've tried to get him into a treatment program or even to an Alcoholics Anonymous meeting but he shrugs it off." Sophia sighed as she sank into the leather seats of Julia's Infiniti. "He thinks *I* have the problem and that I'm too sensitive. I'm sure his drinking was a factor in Jay and Becca's divorce. I actually like her, you know."

"Alcoholism is a huge problem. Most alcoholics don't see themselves as others do and refuse to acknowledge their disease." Julia deftly steered the car into the one-way street. "I'm guessing Jay hasn't admitted he drinks too much."

Sophia scoffed. "Of course not. He never owns the problem. He's quick to find something or someone to blame. The bank. Business. Becca. Me."

"That's too bad," said Julia, making the turn into the street where Sophia's hotel was located. "Do you know if Becca is moving out of town? I heard she might be headed to Seattle."

"Yes, she is. She landed a great job in internal auditing at West Cascades Mutual Saving Bank. She has a degree in accounting and is planning to take the test soon to be a certified public accountant. Her new employer will pay for it, she told me. She'll have a decent income and will be able to keep the boys in private school. She seems excited about it. And her sons will only be a couple of hours from their dad."

"Unless traffic on Interstate 5 gets in the way," said Julia. She turned into the entrance drive of the hotel and stopped in front of the glass doors. "Here you are, Sophia. It was my pleasure to meet you tonight. I hope you feel better in the morning. Good luck to you."

"Thanks again. Ciao." Sophia stepped out of the car and disappeared into the lobby behind the tinted doors.

An interesting evening all around. It almost sounds like Sophia and Becca are best buds, Julia thought to herself as she finished the short drive to her home.

CHAPTER 3

WHO'S GOT THE MONEY?

J ulia woke with a start to the buzz of her alarm Sunday morning. Still half-asleep, she picked up her bedside landline phone, thinking it was the hospital operator calling her. The dial tone hummed in her ear for a few seconds before she realized that her radio was making the sound.

Now fully awake, she tried to remember the number of nights on call that had been as quiet as this one had been. It was a very small number, to be sure. She was hopeful that her 200-bed community hospital would add full-time hospitalists soon. When that happened, if it happened, she could focus on her clinic practice while hospital-based physicians managed her patients when they were hospitalized. She looked forward to nights without interrupted sleep. She surely wouldn't miss having to go into the hospital for critical care unit admissions in the wee hours, then seeing patients all day in clinic.

Julia cruised through her morning rounds, seeing the patients in the critical care unit first as always, followed by those patients who had been admitted the day or night before, then all the other patients starting with the telemetry floor, including Mrs. Benson, who was happy to learn that she was stable enough to be discharged home.

Julia noticed a small stack of going home clothes sitting on the bedside chair and winked at her patient. "I'm writing orders for a two-week follow-up appointment with me," said Julia. "We'll discuss that trip to San Francisco then."

"Of course, Dr. Fairchild." Mrs. Benson clapped her hands. "Thank you so much for getting me well. You're such a blessing to Parkview."

Julia smiled at her sweet, white-haired, grandmotherly patient. "I think I've told you before that coming back to work here wasn't my Plan A. It was my own grandma who encouraged me to consider it just a few months before she died. She kept telling me I would be happy, and she was right. She's probably dancing in heaven right now." She gently patted Mrs. Benson's hand. "Stay out of trouble."

Having finished her duties, Julia conferred with her partner who would take over at noon, and confirmed dinner plans with Alex before slipping out of the hospital and heading home.

JULIA'S DOG bounced and pranced at the door, happy to get some love and attention. Julia changed into gardening clothes comprised of a pair of old jeans and a mangy University of Washington sweatshirt, and collected her bucket of tools. She had promised to help her new neighbor get her yard in shape after years of neglect. The small yard boasted overgrown shrubs, straggly perennials and blooming weeds. Today Julia planned to teach Ellie how to prune the huge *Pieris Japonica* into submission.

"Where did you learn all this about so many plants?" Ellie Collins asked. "I'll never remember all the names."

"You don't have to know it all at once," Julia assured her. "I've learned over the years, first from my mom and grandma starting at about age five. At that age, I thought dead-heading the roses was fun." She laughed. "Now I know better."

"I don't think we had anything but rhododendrons. A lot of them," said Ellie. "My mom said it was because the deer tended to leave them alone."

"You shouldn't have problems with deer in your backyard here in the flats," said Julia. "They can be a nuisance anywhere in the hills, however. I figure they were here first, but I suppose if they were eating my plants I'd think differently."

Ellie pointed to a plant with long stems and chartreuse heads. "Please tell me about this one. Is it a weed?"

"The way it spreads, you'd think so," Julia replied. "This particular plant starts out as a cute little thing with a single stem but grows into a monster bush the next year. It's a biennial, which means it takes two years to mature. The second year it blooms and is quite lovely. Then it throws off millions of seeds and the third year you'll have twenty more of these little darlings growing anywhere they'd like. Its official name is *Euphorbia characias wulfenii,* but it's usually called Mediterranean spurge. I have some smaller varieties with better manners that I can share with you."

Ellie giggled. "You make plants sound like people."

Julia snipped a couple of branches off, gently coaxing the *Pieris* back into a manageable size and shape. "Sometimes I have to remind myself that it's okay to toss plants into the trash when I don't like them anymore. They're not children." She grinned at Ellie. "But I hate to get rid of a living being." She stepped back to see how the shrub looked. "Luckily my sister,

Carly, lives on ten acres in the country and takes pretty much anything I want to discard. It's a symbiotic relationship."

She handed the loppers to Ellie and explained the process of pruning out the limbs that were diseased, damaged, dead or growing in the wrong direction. "Remember that you can't really go wrong here. The plant will grow back and give you a second chance if you don't like how it turns out."

Julia felt the buzz of her pager on her waistband. She always wore it, even when not on call, just in case. It was a convenient way to be reachable when she didn't want to carry her cell phone. She read the short message: CALL SOPHIA 360-694-0000. She was puzzled for a moment then realized it must be the phone number for the Grecian Inn. *Why is Sophia calling me?*

"Excuse me, Ellie. I need to make a call. Back in a minute or two."

"Sophia, what's wrong?" Julia asked, hearing Sophia's sniffles as she answered the phone.

"Oh, Julia. Thank you for calling. I'm not sure what it is but Jay's not answering his phone. I don't have my rental car to check on him because I left it at his house last evening before the gala." Sophia explained. "I don't know what to do. I'm worried."

"Tell you what. Let me wash my hands—I've been playing in the dirt—and I'll come right over and take you to his house. Give me fifteen minutes."

"Thank you. Thank you. I'll wait in the lobby."

Julia promised Ellie that they would continue the horticulture lessons later in the week, then hurried to pick up Sophia. As they drove to Jay's home in an historic part of town with stately homes, Sophia told Julia how she had met Jay.

"I had a small part in a play at the Phinney Street Theatre in San Francisco," Sophia said. "Jay had paid to attend one of the post-show backstage parties and we started talking. We just hit it off." She gave a half-smile and sighed.

"Was he already divorced from Becca?"

"Just about. They were still arguing about some of the final settlement terms, but it was very close to a done deal. I wasn't a factor in the divorce itself."

Sophia confirmed Jay's address as Julia maneuvered through the original Old West Side streets. This was the part of town where the early city developers and business owners had built their homes in the 1920s. Her own house, though stately, was one of the smaller ones, typical of the homes on the outer border of the historic neighborhood. Jay's home was from the same era, but was larger and more impressive. She pulled into the driveway and both women hopped out. They rang the doorbell but Jay didn't answer. After a couple of minutes they walked around to the back, where they found the rear entrance door standing wide open.

"Jay! Jay!" Sophia called as they walked into the house cautiously. Julia saw him first, sprawled out on the floor in the nicely appointed dining room.

"Call 911, Sophia." Julia immediately went into doctor mode and assessed Jay. He was warm, had a thready pulse and was breathing, but barely. His skin was pale. She didn't see any blood. The ambulance and emergency medical personnel arrived within five minutes and took over while Julia told them her initial findings. After performing basic stabilization procedures they whisked him off to the emergency room, with Julia and Sophia following in Julia's car.

WAITING IN THE FAMILY AREA, Julia quizzed Sophia. "When did you last talk with Jay? Did he say he felt ill?"

"He called this morning at about eleven and asked if we

could have lunch together," Sophia replied. "He said he wanted to apologize and would be at my hotel by noon. I called him at twelve thirty when he hadn't shown up yet. He didn't answer so I thought he might be on his way. Fifteen minutes later he still hadn't shown up and he didn't answer again. That's when I got worried and called you."

"What about being sick?"

"No, not that he mentioned," said Sophia. "Although I wouldn't be surprised if he had a major hangover. That would serve him right." She sat back in the chair and crossed her arms, one leg crossed over the other.

"Do you know what he might have done this morning?"

"He said he'd played nine holes this morning and went home instead of playing the back nine because he felt tired."

"Do you know who he played with, or where?"

Sophia thought for a moment. "I think they were at the Pioneer Country Club, but he didn't say who the other guys were. The pro shop should know because it was probably his regular Sunday group. Gene, Terry, and Brian are the names he's mentioned before. One of them might know more than I do."

"That's worth checking out."

Julia caught movement behind the nurse's station and saw Dr. Gorman emerge. He spotted her and motioned for her to join him. Julia cocked her head toward Sophia and raised her eyebrows. When he nodded in return, she took Sophia's hand and led her to the entrance of the patients' area.

"What's the verdict, Paul?" Julia asked.

He pursed his lips and looked at Sophia. "I'm sorry to have to tell you that Mr. Morrison died. We weren't able to resuscitate him despite our best efforts."

Sophia gasped and sobbed on Julia's shoulder. Dr. Gorman and Julia exchanged looks; this was one of the most dreadful parts of their job. They gave Sophia a quiet moment, and when she regained her composure she asked to see Jay. Dr. Gorman had one of the nurses take her into the cubicle for some private time.

"Nice front-line work, Julia," said Paul. "I wish we could save them all."

"Yeah, me, too. I'm curious if you noticed anything that might explain what really happened. Was there evidence of seizures? Unexpected lab results? That sort of thing. I like to hear the rest of the story, as you know."

Paul leaned against the hallway wall, hands in the pocket of his long, white coat. "You saw him at the house, so you know there wasn't any obvious external injury. I didn't find anything either on a more thorough exam once he got here. What I did discover is that he had metabolic acidosis with acute renal failure. My assumption is that the acidosis was so severe it caused shock, leading to cardiac arrest and his death. We worked on him for forty-five minutes but couldn't get any kind of sustained cardiac activity. His medical records in the system didn't identify any obvious triggers for kidney failure."

Julia's antennae quivered. "Really? That's interesting. Any other clues?"

"Clues are for mysteries," Paul chastened. "This is just a medical case, not a detective story. And there weren't any other clues like needle marks or hint of illegal drugs. Medical toxicology results will take a few weeks, but I expect those results will be negative based on what I know so far."

"Okay. Thanks, Paul. His girlfriend is pretty shaken up about this." Julia saw Sophia and the nurse coming back from Jay's cubicle. "There she is now. I'll take her home."

"Thanks. Gotta run. Another ambulance just rolled in. Bye, Julia."

Julia cradled an arm around Sophia's shoulders as they

walked out to the waiting area. She grabbed a couple of tissues from the counter to replace the useless wad of soaked paper in Sophia's hand.

"I'll take you back to the hotel. You might want to make some phone calls."

"Thanks." Sophia managed a few more sniffles.

Julia turned to leave the waiting room and saw two policemen standing inside the doorway.

"Ms. Alder?" the taller one asked.

"Yes, I'm Sophia Alder," she replied, eyes wide. "How can I help you?"

"Hello, ma'am. Hello, Dr. Fairchild. I'm Detective Hughes," he said. "This is Officer Mealy," pointing to the shorter, redheaded man. "We have some standard questions so we can understand what happened at Mr. Morrison's house. With any unexpected death we start an investigation. Is this a good time?"

Sophia replied softly, "As good as any."

"There's a family room down this hall," said Julia. "We can have some privacy there." She led the way to the small room that was most often used when one of the doctors talked to a family about a patient who had died in the Emergency Department.

Sophia answered the officers' questions, which were similar to the ones Julia had asked earlier. She maintained her composure through the process—*like an actress playing a role,* Julia found herself thinking.

After a long twenty minutes, Officer Hughes pocketed his pen and paper as he said, "Ms. Alder, thank you for your time. I'm sorry for your loss. Please stay in town for a few days while we finish our work, although I don't expect any real problems. Good day, ma'am." He turned to Julia. "Dr. Fairchild, do you have any other information?"

Julia was a little surprised to be asked but she *had* been first on the scene with Sophia. She affirmed what Sophia had already said and confirmed her availability if needed.

SOPHIA LOST her composure and started sobbing when she was safely in Julia's car. "Julia! They must think I'm guilty of something. They asked all those accusatory questions. I didn't do this. I loved Jay."

"It's okay," said Julia, patting Sophia's arm. "That's standard procedure. Everyone is questioned in the beginning of an investigation. It helps them establish a timeline of events. It's most likely going to be called an accidental death in the end, caused by a medical condition, from what Dr. Gorman said. How about I get you back to the hotel?"

"Thanks, but first I need to pick up a few things I left at Jay's house, if that's okay. It'll only take a couple of minutes. And I should retrieve my rental car."

Yellow police tape was draped across the front porch and door, which was standing ajar. Julia knocked loudly, then called out when she heard no response. She pushed the doorbell. To her surprise, Detective Hughes and Officer Mealy came to the door.

"Hello—um—officers," Julia stammered. "I didn't expect to see you here. Ms. Alder would like to collect some personal items from the house. Would that be okay?"

The two men looked at each other. Officer Mealy spoke. "I'll accompany her. You can stay here with Detective Hughes."

When Sophia and Mealy were out of earshot, Julia asked for permission to look around. The detective agreed, as long as she didn't touch anything. He knew of her reputation for being honest and easy to work with.

As Detective Hughes resumed filling in his notes, Julia

walked slowly through the main floor of the ninety-year-old house. She admired the elegant millwork, high ceilings, polished oak floors and fine furniture. She assumed that either Jay or Becca, or maybe both, had excellent taste. In the dining room that Jay had apparently been using as a home office she found a disorganized pile of papers on a table and a file cabinet with its four drawers pulled open. *Someone was looking for something. I wonder if they found it.*

She heard footsteps and saw that Sophia had rejoined her, Mealy leaving her as he headed toward the room where Detective Hughes had been. Julia asked Sophia, "Do you notice anything unusual in here? Even if you've only been here a few times, something might catch your eye."

Sophia looked around the room. "That file box is usually in his den, not here in the dining room." She pointed to a charcoal-gray metal container on the sideboard. "I suppose he could have pulled it out to work on something in here."

"Any idea what was in it?" asked the ever-curious Julia.

"Not really, but it seemed like Jay was always looking in it for something."

Julia glanced toward the open doorway to the living room; the detectives were still out of sight. "Well, Sophia, let's look and see if we can figure it out," said Julia as she popped open the lid. Inside she found several manila file folders filled with papers, with one empty file labeled "ESCO—Union." Julia frowned. "Do you know of a connection between Jay and the union at ESCO?"

"A little. Jay mentioned that some of the guys had concerns about unauthorized trading in the pension fund. He said he was trying to figure out how and who was doing it, if it was really happening."

"That's odd," said Julia. "Adam Johns, one of the ESCO union guys, was asking Drake about that last night. I thought

Drake's bank was managing those funds. Why would Jay be involved?"

Julia jumped when she heard a doorbell ring. She quickly closed the file.

Detective Hughes entered the dining room. "You'll need to leave, Dr. Fairchild and Ms. Alder. We are now treating this as a homicide."

CHAPTER 4

CSI PARKVIEW

As had become their Sunday habit, Julia and Alex began their dinner with margaritas at their favorite local Mexican restaurant, Playa Jalisco.

"Does anyone know if Jay has heirs?" asked Julia. "Other than his two sons, that is."

"He has a will on file at our office," Alex replied. "One of my partners was working with him last fall when he and Becca were splitting assets. I don't personally know any details. It will probably be a straightforward process unless there are extenuating circumstances."

Julia sipped on her drink. "I wonder how Becca will make out. She must have gotten a nice share of money at the time, and now her boys will likely get the rest of what he had, considering he was an only child. I heard his parents left him insanely well off."

"That's the common story. Jay never said otherwise to my knowledge."

"I trust your partner did proper estate planning for the boys," Julia mused. "This will be tough on them."

Alex coughed. "The Parkview Theatre is probably slob-bering over the possibility of getting a significant bequest. He seemed to think he could buy his girlfriend some stage time."

"Here in Parkview? How would that help her get famous?"

Alex shrugged one shoulder.

"On another note, I'm dying to know the official cause of death. He died so quickly. For him to have that degree of kidney failure and not to have known earlier, enough for meta-bolic acidosis to kill so quickly, well, that seems unlikely. But it didn't strike me as typical for a heart attack, either. The elec-trocardiogram was normal, according to the emergency doc. But with no evidence of a struggle or an external wound it probably *was* an internal medical condition that killed him. Yet something doesn't sit well with me for this to be a normal death."

"You mean unassisted, don't you?"

Julia raised her glass. "Yep."

Monday morning

Some Monday mornings were harder than others when Julia's alarm went off at 4:45 a.m. so she could do a three-mile run with her Beagle-mix rescue dog. This was one of those. Even Trixie opened one eye and seemed to question the need for the run. Once Julia had her shoes on and leash in hand, however, Trixie raced her to the door.

The pre-dawn sky was crisp and clear. Orion hung like a beacon, still bright with Regel and Betelgeuse shining as they had for time eternal. Julia didn't know many of the constella-tions, but she loved that she could identify a few, Orion being one of her favorites. She wished her own sign, Virgo, was as easy to find. One of her bucket list items was to learn more about the stars and astronomy. Time to take an evening class at the excellent community college eluded her, however, and learning the material from books or online just didn't work for her.

Julia and Trixie settled into a comfortable jog as her mind raced with questions. *Was Jay's death natural or not? And if the latter, who might have assisted him? What was he doing with those ESCO files? How would he have developed acute renal failure so quickly and what caused it?* She finished her run without answers to any of them.

MORNING CLINIC FLEW BY. The precious few minutes between patients were filled with requests from pharmaceutical reps for signatures for samples, reviewing lab and x-ray results, and squeezing in a dictation or two. A phone call interrupted one such dictation.

"Hi, Aunt Julia. This is Nolan," her nephew began. "I hope you can help me."

"Nolan! What a nice surprise! What kind of help?" she asked. "But first tell me about the baby."

Nolan McLean, who worked as a deputy county sheriff, and his wife, Maggie, had recently celebrated the birth of their first child, born on Nolan's birthday.

"She's so big already," Nolan boasted. "And of course, she's amazing. She'll be walking next month. I swear."

Julia laughed. "They do grow up quickly. What do you need help with?"

"Well, this is actually a business call," he said more solemnly. "The Parkview police detectives have asked the county detective staff to help them with the investigation of the Jay Morrison case. They're shorthanded with one of their staff out with an injury for a few weeks."

"Okay. Sounds reasonable."

"I think they asked me to help because of that murder back in February." Nolan had enjoyed a few weeks of local fame after he solved a baffling case of identity theft combined with a cover-up murder.

"That's flattering, Nolan. I knew you'd make your mark as a deputy. So how can I help you today?"

"According to the notes I was given, you were at Mr. Morrison's house when he was found. With you being a doctor and all, I thought you might have more information from your observation skills."

"That might take more than a couple of minutes," said Julia. "I'm taking a lunch break in about twenty minutes. Can you come over to the office? I'll order take-out teriyaki from the place across the street if you'll pick it up."

Nolan arrived at the prescribed time with two orders of chicken teriyaki from Julia's favorite lunch spot. The food was always delicious and served in generous portions.

"This is just what I needed," said Julia, digging in. "What questions have popped up?"

"The initial autopsy report is already back. You already know there wasn't any evidence of external injury but there have been several references to Mr. Morrison saying he didn't feel well earlier in the day. Any thoughts on that?"

Julia took a swig of water. "The obvious one is a major hangover. He was quite drunk Saturday night at the gala. But chronic drinkers don't usually die from that. Sophia said he wasn't feeling well Sunday morning but played golf anyway. Maybe he and his buddies had something to eat or drink at the clubhouse."

"Not that they've reported. They thought he was just hungover, like you said."

"I'm assuming you checked his house for any medications laying around, like Pepto Bismol or Tums."

"We found a bottle of Tums on the bathroom counter, and some ibuprofen. That's all." Nolan took another big bite of his food. "Oh, and a couple of glasses in the sink. They smelled of alcohol. I couldn't place what the drink had been."

Julia's ears perked up. "Two glasses?"

"Yeah. We wondered who used the second glass. Or maybe he used a clean glass for a second drink."

"That doesn't sound like a guy kind of move to me. He'd more likely use the same glass. Less dish-washing later."

Nolan chuckled. "I agree. That's why we're having forensics check them for prints and all."

"CSI Parkview!" Julia raised her water bottle. She was proud of her nephew. He'd been a deputy sheriff for about three years. She knew from her sources that he was well thought of. And very modest.

Nolan's radio went off. "Yes, I'm just finishing up here. I'll be there in ten." To Julia he said, "Gotta run. My real job needs me. Let me know if you think of anything else."

Julia gave him a quick hug as he left. Afternoon clinic went by as quickly as the morning had. She was more than glad to be done a little earlier than usual. The last two days had felt like five. She looked forward to her evening tap class where she could burn a few hundred calories and focus on the dance step combinations instead of Jay's cause of death.

TRIXIE WAS DOING HER "WELCOME-HOME-I'M-HUNGRY" dance as Julia entered through the sunroom door. She was sure sometimes that her dog was saying "Hi, Momma" when her dog howled like a mini-coyote.

Barely three bites into her own dinner of roasted chicken breast and green beans, Julia was interrupted by the beeping of her pager.

"Hi, Sophia. What's up?"

"The police were here asking me a lot more questions," she said between sniffles. "They're acting like they think I killed Jay. I didn't do it. How do I make them believe me?"

"Okay, slow down," Julia said in her calming voice. "What kind of questions?"

"Like where was I after the gala? Would they find my fingerprints on the glass in the sink?" Sophia paused to blow her nose. "And they fingerprinted me! I don't have any kind of record. This is so scary."

"That's standard practice in a situation like this. Tell me more about what happened Saturday when you were with Jay. Take a big breath first."

She inhaled and exhaled loudly and slowly. "Okay. When I got to Jay's house before the gala—I drove my car over because he was going to be busy right up to the last moment—I could tell he was upset and he'd already been drinking. We had a few words over that. He promised to stick to water and coffee at the gala. Of course, that didn't happen. He got noisier and rowdier as the evening went on, as you know. I was totally embarrassed and told him he was too drunk for me to feel safe in the car."

"Why didn't you have me drive you to his house to get your car instead of the hotel?" Julia asked.

"I just didn't think of it at the time."

"On second thought, considering what happened on Sunday, it might be better that you *didn't* go to his house. Tell me more about how he was before the gala. Did he say anything about what had upset him? Had he talked to anyone?"

"I know he was concerned over the pension fund mess. That Adam guy had been at the bank the day before to ask about the union account again and had gotten another bank involved. There might be something there because Jay kept telling him he didn't understand why a large amount of money appeared to be unaccounted for. I guess Adam, Mr. Johns, was very verbal and threatening a lawsuit and all that."

"What about the glass in the sink? Did you handle it?"

"Maybe. We went to the movies Friday evening, and I had a glass of Baileys before we left. He might not have washed dishes, especially if his dishwasher was still full of clean ones. He would have had to empty it first."

Julia chuckled, knowing her own tendency to let the clean dishes sit for a day or two before she put them back in the cupboard. "Anything else you can think of?"

"I don't think so."

"What are your plans now? You mentioned an audition coming up in San Francisco."

Sophia sighed. "I have to stay in town for at least a few more days until Detective Hughes says I can leave."

"Hang tight and stay in touch. I'll keep my ears open."

"Thank you, Julia. You're my only friend around here."

Hardly a friend, Julia thought. However, she certainly could understand how alone the girl might feel with her boyfriend dead and now police hammering questions at her.

WITH A NAGGING SUSPICION that she was overlooking something important, Julia made a list of potential suspects in precipitating Jay's death while she finished her dinner. His ex-wife, Becca, the bank's vice president, Gregory Lantz, and Sophia were obvious choices. She thought she should include someone from the bank's major competitor, Parkview National, as well, where Drake Ashford, Pam's beau, sat at the helm. The two banks competed for the same business accounts in the medium-sized town. Then there was the union who had some concerns, but what benefit would the union—or the others, for that matter—get from Jay's death?

She started to call Nolan but stopped as she reminded herself that she was a doctor, not a detective, and was involved only by happenstance. Instead she called Pam, who hadn't called Sunday afternoon, after all. "How did the visit with your mom and sister go?"

"It was a good thing I got there when I did. Susie was ready to drive off and leave mom alone. She wasn't about to wait for me. She said she'd had it with mom."

Julia pictured Pam making a face. "You've mentioned before that they get on each other's nerves." Julia sipped on a glass of cabernet, her evening treat.

"And the two of them get on *mine*. They're too much alike. Anyway, I was able to hire some in-home help to give Susie a break. And mom finally agreed to look at assisted living apartments. There are seven or eight nice ones not far from her home."

"That sounds like progress. Did Drake tell you that I had fun and games after the theatre gala Saturday night?"

"I meant to ask you about that," said Pam. "I haven't talked to him since I got back last night. Thanks again. I owe you. What kind of fun and games did you have? With ... Drake?"

Julia laughed at the tinge of concern in her friend's voice. "No, not with Drake, no worries there. Technically, it was the day after the gala and I haven't seen it in the paper yet, but Jay Morrison died the next day, as in yesterday."

"No! What happened?"

"Not sure yet. His girlfriend, Sophia, and I found him unconscious at his house on Sunday. He died at the hospital a little later. It's probably a normal death but the police are investigating it as a possible homicide."

"On what basis? Did they find something suspicious?"

"I hadn't thought so, but from my view his cause of death seemed way too sudden and his health records didn't show such issues previously. Plus the back door to his house was open when we got there."

"In October? Maybe he took his trash out and collapsed when he came back in?"

"Yeah, maybe that's what happened."

"Hey, my sister's trying to call. I'd better answer before she sends the police to my door."

"Sure. Talk to you later this week. Good luck with your sister." Julia smiled as she ended the call. Pam always seemed to have a disaster of one kind or another going on. If it wasn't her mother or her sister, it was one of her three kids needing something. And always urgently.

Julia dressed quickly for her Monday evening tap dance class where she had to concentrate on the step combinations. If only she could make her feet remember after that third shuffle-heel-shuffle step to do a brush-back before the flap, she'd have it down pat. Well, almost. Then she had to learn it going the opposite direction to the left, which always seemed harder than going to the right. It didn't leave any room for thinking about murders or anything else.

JULIA DRESSED WARMLY for her morning run. Trixie tolerated the dog-jacket on cold mornings, but always managed to get it off by herself in twenty seconds or less when they got back to the house. The thermometer read 32 degrees—the first morning freeze. The leaves on the path around the lake a short block away crinkled under her feet. Her breath turned into fog in the dry air. She counted a half-dozen fellow runners, some with dogs, at the early hour on the wide path around Lake Sacajawea. She felt invigorated at the end and wished she had a free day to go to the ocean beach, an hour and a half away. Even though it was a cold fall day. She never tired of watching the waves pound the beach. Sometimes Julia envied the people who could take a day off without notice but, for her, rescheduling twenty or more patients was a major task. She got ready for work instead.

ONE OF HER elderly female patients had been admitted to the hospital's orthopedic floor the evening before. Sadie Bate lived alone in an upscale senior living apartment complex. She had fallen and broken her hip. It was an all-too-common scenario amongst the fragile osteoporotic women in their eighties and nineties and sometimes younger. Poor balance and low activity levels were the usual contributing factors, sometimes exacerbated by side effects of many a medication.

Julia was well-liked by the nursing staff and was greeted by the smiles of the crew on the orthopedic wing. They were seasoned and talented, as well as tight-knit. Julia saw a face, however, that she didn't recognize. Sherry, the charge nurse, introduced her to LeAnne, a traveling nurse who would be working there for three months while one of the permanent nurses was out on maternity leave.

"Pleased to meet you, LeAnne. Everyone around here calls me Dr. Julia instead of Dr. Fairchild. Where are you from?"

"Hi, Dr. Julia," LeAnne said, offering a smile and her hand. "I've lived lots of places but I was born in Seattle. My mom still lives there. I try to take jobs that make it easier for me to get up to visit her. Parkview is a lot closer than my last job in Alameda, California."

"I hope you enjoy your rotation here. This is a great group of nurses. Did I understand Sherry to say you would be here for three months?"

"That's what I signed up for, but sometimes contracts get extended. Do you want to know more about your patient with the fractured hip?"

"Yes, thank you. Please begin."

LeAnne launched into the morning update which included Sadie's vital signs, pain control status, and the orthopedic surgeon's comments from his visit earlier. She located the pre-op electrocardiogram for Julia to review, then waited for her to write new orders in anticipation of surgery later that day.

Later that morning in clinic when she had a lull between patients, Julia called her nephew Nolan. She caught him in his patrol car doing his morning drive-arounds in the northern half of the county.

"Hey, Aunt Julia. This new caller ID in our patrol cars is great!"

"Just like at home, huh?" Julia found herself smiling as she thought of boys both big and little and their new toys. "I have a question about your murder case."

"Yeah? Oops. Hang on. Some idiot just made an illegal turn in front of me."

Julia heard a loud horn honk over the phone.

"Sorry about that. Next time he'll get a ticket if I catch him. So what's your question?"

"I was thinking that there might be a connection to those union guys and the pension fund problem. Adam Johns mentioned it and so did the girlfriend, Sophia."

"Yes, and?"

"Sophia mentioned that Jay was frequently looking in that metal file box, like there was something important in it. Have you thought of looking through Jay's files to see if you can find any documentation or correspondence related to Adam Johns? There might be notes or messages in there that help solve the case."

"That sounds reasonable to me but right now we just don't have the manpower to run down every bunny trail. And as of this morning I'm involved in another case that's going to demand a lot of time."

"Would it help if I did the looking for you? I would be happy to help but only with permission. With someone official there, of course."

"I'm sure you know that wouldn't usually be allowed but maybe the sheriff would make an exception for this situation seeing as you found the body. Well, he wasn't dead yet, but almost. Anyway, I'll talk with my boss and see what he says. Okay?"

Julia heard Nolan's walkie-talkie stir to life in the background. "That would be fantastic. Say hi to your wife and daughter for me."

"Will do. Give me a day or two in case I can't catch up with the sheriff today."

"Got it. Ciao. Thanks."

LATER, while munching on her hospital cafeteria salad bar lunch, Julia found herself thinking about Jay and the suspects, if his death turned out to be murder. *Was Becca at the bottom of this? Was her divorce settlement generous enough? Or not? Was someone at Parkview National jealous enough to kill? Did Jay have enemies from whatever his previous life had been on the East Coast? Was Sophia truly innocent or was she a great actress? What had Greg's wife meant about offshore accounts?*

All too soon, Julia's medical assistant, Amie, knocked on her private office door, letting her know that the first afternoon patient was ready to be seen. Sleuthing would have to wait.

. . .

Her landline phone was ringing as she entered the house after work. She answered just as it went to the answering machine and waited out the brief message. "Julia here. Sorry about that."

"Aunt Julia," said Nolan. "I'm glad I caught you at home. Sheriff Harvill talked to the Parkview chief of police and he said he would be happy to talk with you about helping like you asked, if you call him tomorrow at work. He said something about you and a reputation for solving puzzles?"

"I helped him out a while back on another case. That's all. Thanks, Nolan. I owe you."

"This one's on me. Maggie and I appreciate your help with the baby when we call. Let me know if you need anything else."

Happy that she would likely get to search Jay's files, Julia placed a call to Sophia, having gotten a direct cell number for her. "It looks like I might get permission to go inside Jay's house to look for clues. Would you be able to go with me tomorrow evening?"

"I guess so," said Sophia. "It's not like I have a whole lot to do while I'm stuck here."

"Great. I'm not one hundred percent cleared yet. My nephew Nolan, the deputy sheriff who's helping the police, said he's pretty sure I'll get approval tomorrow."

"Sounds good. What will you be looking for?"

"I'm not sure. Something out of place, files that look like they've been rifled, empty folders. I hope to know what it is once I'm there. Your eyes will help because you've spent some time there. How about I call you tomorrow after I talk with the police chief?"

"Sure. I'm game. The sooner I get my name cleared and learn the truth, the better. I want to go home."

Julia had barely finished the call when her phone rang again. She smiled when she saw Alex's name.

"Hi handsome. How's your day been?" Julia settled in her favorite chair in the sunroom. The late-day sun spilled onto the hardwood floor as long, irregular triangles.

"Long," he replied. "Depositions always seem to take an unexpected twist even if they appear to be cut and dried. I feel like someone squeezed all my juice out, and I'm tired. But I wanted to hear your voice."

Julia could almost hear him smiling over the phone. "Hey, I'm always glad to hear yours. Will I see you this week?"

"As a matter of fact, if you're free Thursday, which I know is usually your day out of the office, I could use some company driving up to Olympia. We have some archived files there that I need to go through instead of having them copied and faxed or delivered here."

"I'd love to go if you can wait until I finish morning rounds about nine. Speaking of files, I'm going to go over to Jay's house tomorrow after work if the police chief says it's okay to look through his records there."

"Are you playing detective again? That could be dangerous if Jay was truly murdered."

Julia thought back to her offer to help Nolan. And of times past when she'd tried to help the police out on a case. Well, Alex was right, considering what had happened before. But what was the danger in just getting some information to pass on to the sheriff's department?

CHAPTER 5
WHO'S MELISSA?

The morning air was brisk and refreshing. Julia enjoyed her morning run with Trixie, although she sometimes felt frustrated that even girl beagles seemed to sniff at every bush. Her reward was a healthy dose of Mother Nature and thirty minutes of exercise at the same time.

As she had promised Nolan, she squeezed in a call to the police chief. He was agreeable to letting her go into Jay's house provided a deputy went with her. After agreeing on a time to meet, Julia could hardly wait for her day to be finished so she could pick up Sophia and do her detecting. When she arrived at the house, Sophia in tow, she was pleasantly surprised to see her nephew at the door, ready to let her in.

"Nolan! I'm so happy to see that it's you." Julia introduced Sophia and Nolan to each other, adding that Nolan was her nephew.

"I thought you might be too busy with your other cases to help with this."

"Actually, I'm doing this on my personal time. That was how I got the sheriff to agree." He gave her a smile.

As he unlocked and opened the front door Nolan asked, "Do you have any idea what you're looking for?"

"Not specifically," she admitted. "I hope I know it when I see it." Turning to Sophia, she said, "Let's start in the dining room. That's where we found Jay," she added for Nolan's benefit.

"I probably don't need to remind you that you shouldn't touch or move anything without checking with me first," said Nolan. "Right, Aunt Julia?"

"Just like on television." She winked at him.

For the next several minutes Julia and Sophia walked around the room without touching anything. When Julia got to the four-drawer, oak filing cabinet, she asked for and was given permission to open the drawers. The top drawer labeled A-I was neat and tidy, alphabetized and in order. The second drawer labeled J-P was more interesting. One file labeled Melissa was in the Ls between LBO and Liberty Mutual.

"That's odd. Just a woman's first name? And misfiled," said Julia as she looked at Nolan, who nodded permission to remove the errant file. The folder itself was empty although the bottom was spread out as though it had previously held a substantial number of pages of paper. Frowning, Julia said, "I wonder if the contents have been refiled elsewhere."

The remaining files in the drawer appeared to be intact and in correct order, as did the files in the third drawer labeled R-Z. The fourth drawer was unlabeled and locked. Julia glanced at Nolan with a raised eyebrow and pointed to the oak desk sitting next to the matching cabinet. After he nodded permission she rummaged through the top drawer and found a key that looked promising. Nolan took the key and unlocked the drawer.

Julia, Nolan and Sophia gasped simultaneously at the contents: a Magnum .357 handgun, a sleeve of ammo, and a discolored, legal-sized envelope. Nolan whistled and waved the women away. He donned a pair of latex gloves that he'd pulled from his pocket and carefully checked the gun, which he found to be unloaded. He put the gun and ammo in an evidence bag to go to the forensics lab. The envelope was empty, disappointing Julia most of all. Julia snapped a photo of the return address before Nolan put it into a separate bag.

Julia continued her search in the dining room/office. A file folder labeled ESCO was on the floor under the buffet, its contents strewn. "I'm sure this file wasn't on the floor when we were here last time, Nolan. Someone's been in here." She looked at Sophia, who silently nodded her agreement.

Nolan picked it up and handed it to Julia after she donned latex gloves. She found a few statements from an investment account. Someone had drawn circles in red ink around some of the numbers. With Nolan's permission she snapped a couple of pictures with her phone's camera, then handed it all back to Nolan. A cursory search of the rest of the main floor—living room, kitchen, guest bath and foyer—yielded nothing. Julia peeked into the upstairs bedrooms while Nolan checked the bathroom. All seemed in order.

"Thanks, Nolan," said Julia. "I'm ready to leave. What about you, Sophia?"

"Very ready. This place gives me the creeps." Sophia shivered.

Julia turned to Nolan. "I know the answer is probably no, but will you be able to let me know any results from forensics?"

"It's a criminal investigation, so probably not," he replied.

Julia smiled sweetly. "I know. Just thought I'd ask. Thanks again. I'm looking forward to seeing that baby soon."

In the car Julia and Sophia said at the same time, "Who's Melissa?"

"A first wife? A relative?" asked Julia. "Has Jay ever mentioned that name to you?"

"Never. But we haven't been dating all that long, remember. If it's a first wife, it would be someone before Becca. Maybe she knows who it is."

"Good thought. I'll suggest that Nolan check it out. Or maybe I should just call Becca."

"I thought of something else. I didn't see Jay's laptop anywhere," said Sophia. "It was always on the dining table."

"Could it be at his office at the bank?"

"No, I don't think so. He had a personal laptop that he kept at home. He said he didn't want to take a chance at mingling his work records with his private stuff."

"I'll mention it to Nolan and he can have someone at his office check there anyway. Here's your hotel."

ONCE HOME, Julia used her basic computer search skills to look up the name of the law firm she'd noticed on the envelope. She found the firm with a Seattle address listed but the website indicated it was no longer in business. Undaunted, she decided to ask Alex to trace it when she saw him the next day. Surely the office files would have been transferred to another legal firm.

THE SNOW-COVERED peaks of the Olympic Mountains to the west and Cascade Mountains to the east sparkled in the bright October sun. Alex's law firm had a sister office in the state's capital city, Olympia. An hour and fifteen minutes away by car, it was convenient when they had business involving state government. It also offered the opportunity to pick up other everyday legal cases. Alex traveled there regularly to take his turn staffing the office.

Julia had rehearsed how she would ask Alex to help with her quest to find the missing Melissa files. His first response was, "Why?" followed by, "How did you come up with that name?" She explained the file cabinet and missing file from a folder labeled Melissa, and the empty envelope in a locked drawer.

"Do I need to remind you that you're not supposed to be involved? This is a police matter."

"I know, but I was there practically when it happened and I can't help but be involved, can I?" She smiled innocently when he turned to look at her with narrowed eyes. "How can it hurt to track down that law office? I'll give the detective on the case any information I discover."

Alex's shoulders relaxed. "I suppose that would be okay. I know the police department is shorthanded with the loss of two officers last year and someone now on leave. That's why they're having the sheriff's office step in on some of their cases."

"That's what my nephew Nolan said. You know he's a deputy sheriff, don't you?"

"Yes, I've met him. He seems to be a good guy and willing to go the extra mile. Like you." He turned to Julia with a resigned grin.

"It's genetic, Alex. So will you help me?"

"Of course. You knew I would."

"I hoped." She blew him a kiss.

At the Olympia office Alex gave Julia a list of firms he thought most likely to have absorbed the files of Jensen & Worth, LLC. It was her task to call them and ask if they were the custodians

54

of the defunct law office. Julia rolled her eyes at the long list and hoped it wouldn't take all afternoon. She took court in the second room of the small office and started plodding through the names on the list. She made call after call without success. On phone call number eighteen she hit pay dirt. Fisher & Stuart had the defunct firm's files but the cardboard boxes were stored at an off-site location.

Julia didn't know exactly which files were needed. She took a stab at using the name Melissa Morrison. After promising to look for the records, the receptionist, Sharon Hart, asked for a legal document to release them, if found. Julia thought quickly and realized that the police department would almost certainly accommodate her.

"Let me work on that, Miss Hart, and get back to you in a couple of days. That will give you time to locate them."

"Perfect, Dr. Fairchild. I look forward to hearing from you."

Julia called Nolan to cover her bases in obtaining permission for the files to be released.

"Sure. I don't see how that would be a problem. You can deliver them to me so they stay in the legal chain. What are you expecting to find, anyway?"

"I'm not sure but there has to be some reason Jay kept that old envelope other than sentimental reasons."

THURSDAY EVENING

Julia wandered around in her own Old West Side home a block from the banks of the town's beloved Lake Sacajawea. It had been built in the early days of the city by one of the executives of the then-new lumber mill. Her father had worked at the mill as a lumber grader in his younger days before he began a career with the postal service. She loved the hardwood floors of yellowed oak, the mahogany cabinets and trim work, and the Italianate styling of the arches on the main floor. She sometimes pretended to be an old-fashioned debutante and walked gracefully down the grand staircase into the foyer with its marble floors where her handsome escort would be waiting. It was a small home but grand in detail. She loved being its owner and caretaker.

She sipped on a second glass of cabernet, relishing her free evening after spending the daytime hours with Alex. He had a legal review meeting every other Thursday evening. She was happy to have time to herself, even as much as she liked him. She had been single long enough to value her personal space. A brief marriage right out of college hadn't worked out. She recalled that her father had said, "It's not too late to back out, you know," when they had stood in the apse ready to walk up the aisle. Had he known it wouldn't work out? She entertained the idea of marrying again, someday, but only when and if the right guy came along. Was it Alex?

She smiled wistfully as she thought of Josh, with whom she'd spent a couple of weeks in Paris in the spring. Everything about him had been right except for his living and working on the East Coast. He had also started seeing someone else in the six months between her seeing him in Amsterdam and later in Paris. She sighed and sank down in her favorite wing chair in front of the fireplace in her den. The chair had belonged to her grandma and was now enjoying new life with buttery-soft, cream-colored leather upholstery.

Julia loved to travel and often persuaded her younger sister Carly to go on adventures with her. Spain was on her list for a future visit, although she would avoid bullfights. Seeing one in Mexico had been enough for her. Perhaps she would make a trip to London instead and tour the gardens. One of her elderly patients who had been born in England had suggested such an excursion during a recent office visit. Or maybe they would take a trip to the British Virgin Islands in February when the weather was so dreary in Parkview. Thinking of her sister prompted her to pick up the phone and call.

"Hey, Carly. What are the chances you could scoot up to Seattle with me on Monday? Would you be able to take a day off work?" Her sister worked in the accounting department at ESCO.

"And why would I want to go to Seattle?"

"Because you love sorting through cardboard boxes while you pretend you're searching for pirate treasure."

"Whose cardboard boxes are you talking about? And what pirate treasure?"

"It's like this. I have a request in to a law firm in Seattle to locate legal files that came from another firm that's closed. I'm fairly certain I'll have to do my own search through the boxes because why would they use their own employees?"

"Makes sense. What are you looking for? What does it have to do with pirate treasure?"

"Do you remember Jay Morrison?" Julia asked. "He started that new bank a few years ago."

"Yeah, sorta. I didn't know him myself but some of the guys were talking about him at the union hall last week. Rob told me at dinner that he died or something."

"He definitely died—no something about it. Although he may have had help."

"Are you getting me into another of your detecting schemes? I don't want any part of it if you are."

"Not really. The only mystery I have is an empty manila file labeled Melissa and an old envelope from a former Seattle law firm. Nolan said I could help to track down anything related to those items."

"*Our nephew* Nolan? Why is he involved?"

"Parkview police are short-handed, and he got volunteered from the Sheriff's department to assist in the investigation."

"I don't like investigations. You always end up in trouble. Like in Amsterdam. And in Paris."

Julia laughed. "I'm just helping with this envelope. I promise. The police aren't going to use official resources to send anyone up there. Please? I would love to have you ride shotgun. It's a long two and a half hours when I go by myself."

Julia heard a loud exhalation before Carly said, "Well, okay. Rob's on swing shift next week so he'll be gone till midnight every day anyway. I have some overtime banked that I can use. But you'll owe me. Again."

"Thanks. I'll give you more details when I firm it up." Julia sat back in the chair, legs curled under her. Trixie lay sleeping in her dog bed between Julia's chair and the fire. Julia smiled, anticipating the potential excitement of finding anything related to Melissa, whoever she was. Or is. She wasn't certain the empty file folder and the aged envelope were related, but had an inkling they were, somehow.

CHAPTER 6

FOLLOWING THE CLUES

Julia swung by the orthopedic unit to see Mrs. Bate, who had breezed through the pinning of her fractured hip and was ready for discharge to a rehab facility. LeAnne handed Julia the requisite discharge order sheets and transfer paperwork while briefing her on the patient's status.

"How are you liking our hospital?" Julia asked as she filled in the forms.

"St. Jerome is a welcoming place," said LeAnne. "I love working with the orthopedic staff. And the doctors are more pleasant than at some of the hospitals where I've worked. They treat me like I actually know how to do my job." She smiled and winked. "I'm considering moving here and applying for a full-time, permanent position. It's close enough to my mom to help her when she needs me. And I'm getting tired of traveling."

"That's good to hear," said Julia. "A lot of the hospital's employees stay here for thirty years and longer."

"I'll get your patient ready for transfer, Dr. Julia. Have a great day."

. . .

Julia's morning clinic was on the light side, but it was a Friday and the weather was good. In the Pacific Northwest, that was often reason enough for people to take a long weekend off work and cancel appointments. Maybe some of her patients were going camping one last time before the weather turned wet and gray for the rest of fall and winter. She stepped out of exam room number three to find Nolan waiting in the hallway, hat in hand.

"Hi, Aunt Julia," he said. "Do you have a minute?"

"Sure. Just a sec while I give Amie instructions for this patient. You can wait in my office two doors down behind me." She cocked her head in the general direction.

Nolan sat on the edge of the extra chair in her office with his toes tapping impatiently. Julia closed the door behind her. "What's going on? You look like a man on a mission."

"Yes, I kind of am. Detective Kilkelly—he's in charge of the Morrison case for the police department—asked me to deliver the autopsy report to you. He said it's because the coroner doesn't have a medical degree and you're already involved. Anyway, he'd feel better if you had a look at this and tell him what it means." Nolan handed a manila envelope to Julia. "His direct phone number is right there on the outside."

"Let's check it out." Julia thumbed through the several pages of medical terminology. "Basically, in layman's terms, Mr. Morrison had a condition called cardiomyopathy. That means a heart that doesn't pump as well as a normal heart. It's larger than normal with weaker muscle. It's a flabby heart."

"Is that why he died?"

"Well, people—more often men than women—do die from it, but Jay, Mr. Morrison, also had methanol found in his blood according to the lab results. That's definitely not normal. Methanol when metabolized in the body becomes a highly toxic acid. It likely resulted in his metabolic acidosis, which means so much toxin was in his system that his kidneys failed. Which then led to his heart failing." Julia looked up from the papers at her nephew. "That's probably what killed him."

"What is methanol used for? I don't think I've ever heard of it."

"It's a type of industrial-use alcohol which is mostly used to create fuel, solvents and antifreeze."

"How would he get methanol in his blood? Intravenously?"

Julia shook her head. "Probably not. Most often it's taken by mouth. Accidentally in some cases and on purpose in others."

"It sounds like we need to look for a source of methanol at the house."

"If someone used it to poison him, they probably didn't leave it behind," said Julia. "Weren't there some glasses in the sink? Have they been tested for anything besides fingerprints?"

Nolan pulled out pen and a notepad. "I'll find out. Ms. Alder said she didn't have a drink with Jay that night before the gala and there were two glasses. Do you suppose there's something in one of his liquor bottles?"

"Only if his visitor left it behind. But it's something to look for. Do you want me to call the detective about this report?"

"He'd like that. He may have more questions for you. I'll get started on finding a source for the methanol." Nolan put his hat on and stood to leave. "Thanks, Aunt Julia."

"No problem." She gave him a quick hug and followed him out the door to see her next patient. "Have you checked out the golfing buddies? Maybe Jay mentioned something to them about a visitor the night before."

"Good idea. Thanks."

"One more thing, Nolan. Remember that empty file folder and the envelope from the house?"

"Of course. What about them?"

"I've tracked down the law firm and am going to Seattle on Monday, so I'll need that letter to give me permission to look. Can you get it to me by then?"

"I'll take care of it today and fax it to you here. Will that work?"

"You're a doll. Thanks." Julia pecked him on the cheek.

JULIA CALLED Alex during her lunch break. "I thought you'd want to know the autopsy findings on Jay."

"You have them already? How so?"

"Detective Kilkelly sent them over with Nolan to see what I thought. It looks like a homicide after all."

"How can you tell?"

"Unless he was suicidal, which doesn't seem likely, it looks like he ingested methanol. That would have caused the kidney failure and probably aggravated his heart condition."

"You probably shouldn't be telling me this, Julia, although the issue of confidentiality goes away with death."

"And you said he was a client in your office."

"He was my *partner's* client but Jay had conferred with me about setting up a trust."

"Do you know if he revealed any medical conditions, like an enlarged heart?"

"That's news to me, but my partner would know more than I do. Would that have caused his death?"

"Maybe eventually, but he had kidney failure as well. Methanol probably triggered it and that's what I think he died from."

"So you're saying somebody helped him, so to speak."

"I'd say so."

"Okay, then. I'll let Peter know when he gets back on Monday. Are we on for dinner tonight? My treat."

Julia chuckled. "You always say it's your treat. When do I get to buy you dinner?"

"It's a treat for me when you cook. It's a guy thing to buy dinner."

"Alright. You win. This time. See you about six."

Julia brushed up her knowledge on acute methanol poisoning in her medical resources online. She didn't think Jay poisoned himself, even accidentally. *Where had it come from?* she asked herself. *How did someone get Jay to drink it?*

Amie broke her reverie when she poked her head in and said, "Mrs. Conner is ready in room one."

THE SELECTION of restaurants in Parkview seemed tilted in favor of Mexican food. Julia had eaten at most of them, ever hoping for the perfect flauta with guacamole and sour cream, home-made-style Spanish rice, and a margarita with just the right combination of lime and sweetness. Playa Jalisco was her favorite place, having won her over with the best margaritas in town, in her opinion. It had proper decor and was on the small side, but the owner and his son knew good food and service.

Alex and Julia felt lucky to score a table inside the main section, considering the hour. They toasted each other as usual when their margaritas on the rocks were served.

"Your brain is somewhere else tonight," said Alex. "Every time I say something, you say huh and I have to repeat myself. What's on your mind?"

Julia set her glass down and leaned forward, elbows on the table. "Who wants Jay dead?"

Alex rested his chin on his free hand while taking tortilla

chips with his other. "Hm. Most likely someone who stands to benefit from his death, as in his heirs."

Julia shook her head. "I can't see Becca doing that. She's already got a divorce settlement. Her boys will eventually inherit much of the estate anyway, I would guess. She's too obvious a suspect. Name someone else." She held the big glass in both hands to take a salt-infused swallow of her drink.

"I haven't seen his will yet. Peter will schedule a reading this week, I'm sure. Jay could have siblings or other relatives."

"As I recall from the newspaper story when he started the bank, he was an only child. They don't usually have siblings." She grinned.

"Touché," Alex replied with a mock salute. "Here's our dinner."

Julia took a bite of her chicken enchilada ranchera. "Yum. Maybe this Melissa person is important enough to be in the will."

"Have you heard back from that law firm yet?"

"Oh, yes. I forgot to tell you. They have about thirty boxes of records waiting for me. I'm going to drive up on Monday with Carly. I have a comp day to use because of working last weekend. We should be there by mid-morning if we get out of here at a decent time."

"It's going to take some time to go through that many boxes."

"That's why I asked Carly to go with me. She's always fun even when we're doing drudge work like this. I promised her a glass of wine when we're done."

"I would have held out for more than that."

"I'll give her a whole bottle." Julia giggled. "Something else. There were some loose bank statements from the ESCO account on the floor at Jay's house. Some of the numbers were circled in red. I thought the union was using Drake's Parkview

Bank for their business. Do you know anything about a switch?"

"I'll ask Drake on Monday. Did you notice the dates on them?"

Julia pulled out her phone and scrolled to the photo gallery. "I took a couple of pictures so I could study them later. Here they are. One is dated July 31 of last year and the other one is August 31 of this year." She showed the screen to Alex.

Alex raised an eyebrow as he glanced at the photos.

Julia continued. "Adam Johns, the union guy, mentioned something about the account when I was with Drake at the gala. Maybe there's something there."

"A random bank statement isn't much help," said Alex.

"Sophia said his laptop was missing at the house. Nolan is going to check with Jay's bank in case he left it at his office."

"Julia, don't you have enough to do with your medical practice? Do you have time to get more involved with this mess?"

Julia smiled at him and said, "Being a doctor is basically the same as being a detective. We follow the clues to figure out a patient's diagnosis or cause of death, as the case may be. I'm just following clues." She punctuated her comment with a swallow of her drink. "Will you let me know what you find out from Drake?"

Alex rolled his eyes. "Sure. Do you think we can finish this meal without any more detective talk?"

"That reminds me. I forgot to call detective Kilkelly about the autopsy report. Maybe he'll be available tomorrow."

CHAPTER 7

TARGET PRACTICE

Julia met Pam at the entrance to the weekly Saturday market at the fairgrounds. It was the last scheduled market day of the season which ran from mid-March to late October. Local vendors offered fresh produce, home-made bread, plants, and all kinds of creations from wood workshops and sewing machines. Julia liked to support the purveyors while enjoying the freshest of vegetables and fruit, in addition to buying a bouquet of fresh flowers to enjoy all week. She and her friend made it their Saturday morning habit unless she had weekend call or clinic. They followed it with a mug of hot chocolate at Julia's house.

"How's your mom getting along now? Did Susie find a retirement home for her?" Julia plated some snickerdoodle cookies while she warmed the milk for the cocoa. She found a vase for the flowers and let Pam arrange them.

"Susie said there were two really good options not far from where mom lives now. That would make it easier for her friends to visit—at least those who still can. Her closest friends are almost as limited in getting around as she is. Yum. This is delicious. Did you slip some Baileys in it?"

"I certainly can do that," said Julia. She found the bottle in the cupboard and handed it to her friend. "Will you have to drive up and look at the homes with your sister?"

"No. I trust her to make that decision. She has power of attorney anyway and knows the area better than I do. I've lived away from Seattle for too many years to be very helpful."

"Changing topics," said Julia as she topped off the mugs. "Has Drake said anything about the union guys and their deposits at his bank?"

"He's closemouthed about it. The only time I've heard him say a word was when I overheard him talking with that Adam guy a few months ago after the account was transferred to River City. Drake said something about not being aware of any improper use of funds."

"Hm. At the gala Adam came up to Drake and mentioned the account. Why would he be talking to Drake when the money is at Jay's bank now?"

"No idea. It wouldn't work that way in *my* business. We would make a clean cut and not look back."

"The pulp and paper business may be more cut and dried than a bank's business." Julia dipped the last of her cookies in her hot chocolate. "It's rarely so neat and tidy in the medical world."

"You have a point. I don't know for sure what goes on in the executive offices." Pam slurped the rest of her drink. "Thanks. Gotta run. I told Susie I'd take care of some business things for her while she and mom traipse around Seattle."

JULIA HAD an unscheduled afternoon to herself. Alex was golfing in a late-season benefit tournament out of town. Sophia came to mind as she ruminated on what Pam had said about the union money. She wondered if that was at the bottom of Jay's murder, after all. Julia thought of Sophia being stuck in town for another few days and picked up her phone.

"Hi. I thought I'd see if you feel like getting together. I have some free time on my hands today."

"I'm so bored. I'd love that. Shall I meet you somewhere?"

"We can grab a lunch and drinks at the Back Door Office if you like. It's on Washington Way near the Tenth Avenue intersection."

"I know where that is. I saw it when Jay and I were driving across town one day. Twenty minutes?"

"Perfect." Julia hoped Sophia knew something more about Jay's recent encounters that might help identify his murderer. She knew Alex would tell her to stay out of it, but she was only helping Nolan, wasn't she?

"THANK you so much for inviting me out. I was going nutso in that room. I've watched all the reruns of *The Closer* and *Blue Bloods* I can handle." Sophia sipped on her lemon drop cocktail as she perused the menu offerings. "Yum. The bartender knows how to make a great drink." She glanced around the room. "This looks like a great cocktail bar. It's similar to some fun places I enjoy in San Francisco."

Julia followed Sophia's eyes, taking in the upscale decor with smoky glass, brushed nickel metal accents, black leather chairs and benches, and black high-top tables for two. It looked stark in the daylight yet still felt intimate with its cozy seating arrangements.

She raised an eyebrow. "You mean there's something in Parkview worthy of your praise?" She saluted Sophia with her glass of crisp, chilled pinot grigio.

Sophia laughed. "I know I was acting like a snob at the gala last weekend. Please forgive my boorish behavior. I've since learned to appreciate some things about this town—-you, for example."

"Thank you for that. If you stay in Parkview long enough you'll discover that we have pretty much everything that's necessary for a good life, but without the traffic congestion and long commutes of big cities. I go to Portland, for example, once in a great while for upscale shopping but I wouldn't want to live there. I can get to my office within seven minutes and all the way across town in less than fifteen. Unless I have to wait more than one cycle at a traffic light."

"I get it," Sophia said as she signaled to the waiter to take their orders. "My treat today."

"How much longer do you have to stay in town, or do you even know yet?"

"Jay's attorney, Peter Lewis, called and said he would arrange for a meeting to read the will next week. He was saying Wednesday looked good. I'd like to get it over with. I don't expect Jay to have left me anything, but Mr. Lewis said I had to stay."

"Did he say why?"

"No. Detective Kilkelly said the same thing." Sophia sighed. "I hope I still have a chance at that part when I finally get to go home. My agent said they've delayed the filming and I can still audition—if I ever get back home!" Sophia snorted. "I was supposed to be back in San Francisco last Monday, but, well, you know the rest of the story." She took a bite of her shrimp and asparagus salad. "Wow. This is delicious."

"And right here in Parkview," said Julia. "The chef grew up across the river on a lavender farm. He said he always wanted to own a restaurant. After he went to culinary school in New York he came back to fulfill his dream. Way too expensive on the East Coast, he said. Lucky us." Julia speared a forkful of her own dish. "This spinach salad with grilled chicken and marinated green beans is excellent. I wish I had more time during my lunch break to run over here and enjoy this more often. Cafeteria salads at the hospital are a dismal second to this."

"Have you talked with Nolan recently? Does he have any more information about Jay?"

"As a matter of fact, he came by the office yesterday and let me read the autopsy report. Did Jay mention any heart issues to you?"

"No. He told me he was healthy and planned to live to be as old as his dad, who was in his eighties when he died. Why?"

"He had a heart condition he might not have known about. But, and I know you're going to ask, it probably didn't cause him to die."

"What did, then?" Sophia furrowed her brow. "Did the autopsy reveal anything more?"

"He had methanol in his bloodstream."

"Methanol? Is that rubbing alcohol?"

"No. That's isopropyl alcohol. Methanol is used mostly in industries, like our local pulp and paper business."

"Where would he have gotten it? He doesn't work in the paper mills."

"That is the question of the day. I suggested that Nolan look in Jay's liquor cabinet in case something was spiked with it. And to test those glasses that were in the sink if they still had them."

"But how would it kill him?"

"It causes the kidneys to shut down if you drink enough of it. That may be why he didn't feel well Sunday morning. He likely drank it, unbeknownst to him, sometime in the 48 to 72 hours before he collapsed."

"Well, we had dinner Friday night at The Oyster House but

he took me back to the hotel early so he could work on his remarks for the theatre gala the next evening. I cooked at his house Thursday night. I'm sure I didn't use any methanol in the chicken marsala." Sophia managed a grim smile.

"Did he say he was meeting anyone else Friday after he dropped you off?"

"No. He seemed worried, though, about some last-minute changes and cancellations that could affect raising enough money to meet the goal."

Julia's antennae twitched. "Do you know more about those? As in who canceled out?"

"No. I wouldn't have known them by name, anyway. At least I don't think I would have. Are you thinking something sinister was going on?"

"I admit I find it curious."

Sophia took care of the check while Julia answered her phone, noting that it was her friend, Pam.

Julia heard sobbing. "What's wrong?"

"It's Drake! Someone drove by his house and shot out the glass in his front door."

"Is he hurt? Were you with him?"

"He's okay, he said. I'm on my way and he called the police. Can you meet me there?"

"Um. Okay. Give me the address and I'll be there soon. Bye."

Sophia asked, "Is *who* hurt?"

"That was Pam. Someone shot out Drake's front door glass."

"Is there a vendetta against bankers around here?"

JULIA SAID her goodbyes to Sophia, then drove to Drake's home on Parc Hill. The neighborhood sprawled over the eastern ridge of Cascade Heights. The roads seemed to go every which way but the right way. Julia got turned around a couple of times before she found Drake's home, which turned out to be a mid-century multilevel structure with the front entrance on the second level. She walked across an elevated walkway over a koi pond to the front door, where a uniformed policeman checked her identification, talked into his shoulder mike, then waved her in.

Nolan stood in the living room next to Officer Mealy. Drake leaned against the back of the ultra-modern davenport, face ashen. He turned when he heard Julia's heels click on the wood floor. "I thought you might be Pam." He sagged further into the cushion.

Nolan indicated that Julia should sit down, so she sat on the edge of the chair next to the end of the coffee table. "I just talked with her. She's on her way. I got here first because I was already closer when I got the call."

"Thanks." Drake reached for the glass of water on the table. The contents sloshed on the wood surface as he tried to take a drink. "I can't believe this has shaken me so much. I'm not even physically hurt."

Nolan said, "We found a bullet embedded in the door of the coat closet in the foyer. Pretty small caliber and probably from a commonly available gun. We'll let forensics have at it. I don't have any more questions for you right now, Mr. Ashford. Officer Mealy and I will canvass the neighbors and see if anyone saw or heard anything, but in this neighborhood I don't expect much. Your neighbors are too far away."

Drake walked to the door with the two men. "Thanks, officer. I'm sure you'll do your best." He started to close the door but paused when he saw Pam running across the walkway. He waited while she slowed to acknowledge the officers, then picked up her pace and swooped into the house.

"Drake! You're okay! I was so scared you might be injured."
She threw her arms around him and whimpered.

Drake held her close for a moment before he walked across
the room to a wet bar and opened a bottle of Capstone
sangiovese. He poured it into three glasses and offered it to
each of the women.

"I suppose you want to hear what happened," he said.

Pam and Julia held up their glasses and nodded.

Drake sat on the davenport next to Pam and patted her
arm. "I'd been in my office for a couple of hours looking at the
statements that Mr. Johns gave me from when the union
pension account was at River City Bank. Some interesting stuff,
by the way. Anyway, I heard a motorcycle outside. It caught my
attention because I don't usually see or hear them up here. I
don't know anyone who owns one on this street."

"It could have been someone out for a spin. The streets up
here might be a fun challenge for some of those dudes," said
Julia.

"That's what I was thinking. Then a couple of minutes later
it went back down the hill, at least I thought it was probably
the same one. A few seconds later I heard glass breaking at the
same time that I heard the cycle rev and speed away."

Pam covered her mouth in horror. "What if you had been
standing at the door?"

"Well, I *wasn't* and I can repair a window. I don't have
much hope that the culprit will be found."

"Did you wonder if it's related to Jay Morrison?" Julia
asked. "You're another banker, after all."

He frowned and paused a moment. "No, it didn't cross my
mind. Why on earth would I think that? He wasn't shot at." His
face darkened as he took a large swallow from his Waterford
wine glass.

Pam said, "It could be hoodlums out causing a ruckus."

"That would be one way to shake up a perfectly good afternoon," said Julia. "This is really good wine, by the way."

Drake smiled and said, "I needed a reason to open this bottle. I've been saving it for a special occasion."

Julia narrowed her eyes at his choice of words.

CHAPTER 8

PLAYING TWENTY QUESTIONS

J ulia was thankful that Lady Luck was with them as she
and her sister Carly made the drive north to Seattle
Monday morning. They cruised through Olympia
without incident, having missed the five-car pileup that
occurred behind them right after they passed Tumwater. The
morning slowdown near Joint Base Lewis McChord was a
breeze compared to typical commute mornings. The north-
bound congestion between Tacoma and Seattle had already
dissipated by the time they got that far.

Sharon, the receptionist with whom Julia had spoken
earlier, greeted them with a big smile at the main desk when
Julia introduced herself and Carly. She noted and accepted the
documentation for checking the files. "Welcome. I guessed
that you two must be related. You have the same nose and
cheekbones."

The sisters looked at each other, having heard similar
comments many times before. Julia and Carly were of Finnish
descent and had the high cheekbones associated with their
inherited genes. Julia, the taller of the two and older by a mere

four years, sported a bouncy brunette bob and blue eyes, courtesy of their father. Carly had inherited the honey-blonde locks, hazel green eyes and sassiness of their mom. Their noses were identical, as were their general facial features.

Sharon opened the gate between the waiting area and her desk. "Come on in. There are thirty-two cardboard file boxes waiting for you in the conference room." She led the sisters down a hall lined with photos of mostly men. They were identified as partners and associates of the law firm. Julia spotted three women in the line-up of about twenty people. Sharon nodded at a couple of men standing in the hallway at an open office door. "A couple of our tort attorneys," she said as the passed them and said, "Good morning."

She stopped in front of a door labeled Conference Room A. The lights turned on automatically as the three women filed into a large room with a huge, oval, conference-style table that was covered with file boxes. "I had our staff pull all the files for the years you requested. You'll notice that there's more than one box for many of those years. I hope you find what you're looking for. I'll keep you supplied with coffee. You'll find a couple of legal tablets and pens on the table. I thought they might be helpful. Let me know if you need anything else." She smiled pleasantly as she turned and left.

"Well, Miss Amateur Detective," said Carly, brushing her blonde curls off her neck, "where do you think we should start?" She waved her hand at the piles of boxes. She slipped off her coat and perused the dates on the boxes closest to her. "This one is dated 1969." She lifted the lid and scowled after looking inside. "Oh, brother. These don't appear to be in alphabetical order. This may take a while."

"We have all day and—here comes Sharon with coffee." Julia shrugged off her jacket and accepted the two steaming mugs. "We can either start in the middle and go both ways, or start at the outside years and move in. What do you think?"

"Starting in the middle seems more logical to me. Did you say you asked for records ten years either side of Jay's birth year? Why?"

Julia removed the lid of the box in front of her labeled 1980. "That envelope at Jay's house was dated 1981. Jay was born in 1979. If our mysterious Melissa is a sibling, I figure she was born within ten years of his birth, considering his parents' age and all that."

"You're totally guessing, sis. You don't even know if she *is* related to Jay. But it's as logical as anything else, I suppose." Carly whisked through a dozen random files in the box labeled 1979. "I'll go through boxes from the earlier years starting with this one and you go the opposite direction. Okay? I assume I'm looking for files that say either Melissa or Morrison. Right?"

"Yes, for now. Maybe we'll get lucky and there'll be a file labeled with both names."

The only sounds in the room for the next thirty minutes were of fingers thumbing through the files, an occasional sneeze caused by the dust on the tops of the boxes, and a giggle now and then when an amusing file came to light. "Why would there be a file for Larry the Clown, for Pete's sake?" asked Carly. "I wonder if anyone cares about confidentiality laws, considering that we're going through these files."

"That's a reasonable thought, but if Sharon's not going to worry about it neither am I," said Julia. "What year are you searching through now?"

"Nineteen seventy-eight. It would sure be helpful if these folders were in some kind of order inside the box. I'd fire the secretary who did this if she worked for me." Carly sneezed again.

"This box is labeled 1980. Nothing interesting so far. I'm

surprised there wasn't anything, considering that was when Jay was born."

"A birth doesn't automatically trigger a file in a law firm, in my opinion. Unless maybe it's an event like Arnold Schwarzenegger's problems a few years back."

Julia chuckled. "Touché."

Another quiet hour passed. "Are you getting hungry yet?" Carly asked. "I'm down to 1976 without anything worth reporting. What about you?"

"I'm still in 1982." She groaned. "There are *three* boxes for this year. Must have been a busy one. I sure thought I'd find something in the 1981 because of that envelope I found." Julia wiped her brow with the sleeve of her sweater. "I wonder if there's another name that we should be looking for."

"And how would we know that name? And who would we ask?" Carly closed the lid of the 1976 box. "I'm ready for lunch. You're buying."

"Of course. Sharon can recommend a place, I'm sure, then we can tackle these boxes again."

THE CAFE in the downtown Nordstrom store was busy but efficient. The wait staff took care of their order and delivered their iced tea promptly.

Julia sat with her chin on her hand, elbow on the table, looking up at the modern brass-trimmed glass ceiling fixtures in the brightly lit space. "What kind of letter would Jay's parents have received in 1981? Would it have been communication about preparing a will now that they had a child?"

Carly scoffed. "Do normal people do wills right after a child is born? It seems to me that most people don't even start to talk about wills until they're in their later years, unless something has happened that makes them worry about inheritance issues."

"I bet you're right. I know many of my patients don't think of a will until they're well into their seventies." Julia paused as the young lady delivering their salads made an appearance. "So that makes me even more curious about what transpired in 1981 that required a letter. And why Jay kept the envelope."

"We have quite a few boxes left to go, sis. I hope the answer is in one of them." She took a bite of her green salad with chicken breast, cold asparagus, and Parmesan crisps. "This is heavenly."

The sisters resumed their search for clues after the refreshing lunch. Carly thumbed through the files in the boxes labeled 1974 and 1975. Julia had finished searching the boxes labeled 1982 through 1983 without finding anything worth mentioning. Sharon popped in every hour or so to refresh their coffee, smiling each time as she exited the room. "Having fun, ladies?" she asked shortly after three p.m. with an impish look on her face.

Julia smiled with clenched teeth in response.

At three thirty Julia whooped and slapped the table. "I think I've found something that might be related."

"Tell me more," said Carly.

"This is a letter from the attorney, a Mr. Maxwell Jensen, to William J. Morrison, who is presumptively Jay's father, dated June 8, 1984." Julia skimmed the letter. "It talks about an account that has been set up at Old National Bank in Bellevue for the purpose of disbursement of funds for the care and education of Melissa LeAnne (Carlton), child of Gloria Taylor Carlton of Seattle."

"That sounds like Melissa could be an illegitimate child," said Carly.

"It sure does. Perhaps Jay isn't an only child, after all," said Julia. "Of course, now we have to track down this Melissa."

"Or her mother. She might be easier to find."

"Unless she's changed her name a few times or moved, or both." Julia shuddered at the prospect of having to trace her whereabouts. "*But*, my dear sister, we don't have to do the work. Nolan and the police department have the resources that can do that." Julia sat back in the office chair. "How about we skim through the rest of these boxes and keep an eye out for the names of Gloria or Melissa Carlton?"

"What about the envelope being dated 1981? That wouldn't go with *this* letter, would it?"

"Maybe there was another letter from 1981 about something else that we didn't find."

"I'd believe that, with the haphazard shape these files are in."

Julia smiled. "I suppose that once the firm closed, whoever prepared these for storage didn't worry so much about them ever being opened again. We should consider ourselves lucky we found anything useful."

"Amen to that. Let's get done with these so we can go home."

"I'll go ask Sharon to copy these files for Nolan and be right back."

JULIA LEANED back in her wing chair in front of the fireplace, stockinged feet on the hassock, Trixie at her side, and a glass of cabernet in hand. She felt she deserved it after the hairy drive home from Seattle. How the citizens of Seattle tolerated their daily commute was a mystery to her. Traffic had increased exponentially since her days in college at the University of Washington. Of course, at that time in her life she had lived in the dorms and didn't drive the freeway to visit home, which was usually only over quarter breaks. It was more convenient to travel by train. She didn't even have the energy to go to her Monday evening dance class, although usually she wouldn't miss it for anything.

After checking for anything important in her private email, she dialed Alex's number.

"Guess what I found out in Seattle today," she said when he answered.

"Are we playing twenty questions?" he teased.

"I hope it doesn't take you that many to figure it out."

"So you must have found something interesting and it relates to Jay. Am I close?"

"Bingo. First, I want to ask if there's going to be a problem of confidentiality if I tell you."

"Probably not. These files are about forty years old. Right?"

"Yes. But what if the person in question is still alive? Is it still okay?"

"It might depend on if there's a criminal act or something illegal involved," said Alex. "But in general, you're probably safe with files that old. You can tell me. I'm not going to report you, anyway."

"Thank you for that. What if I told you that Jay has a sister —excuse me, half-sister?"

"Really? He was an only child according to the news stories several years back. What exactly did you find?"

Julia sat up straighter in her chair. "Well, there's a letter that was written in 1984 from an attorney, a Mr. Maxwell Jensen, to William John Morrison that mentions a bank account set up on behalf of Melissa LeAnne, daughter of Gloria Taylor Carlton. Sounds like a love child to me." She clicked her tongue.

"You could be jumping to conclusions. Maybe this Gloria is

a sister and Melissa is a niece and Mr. Morrison was helping her out. Jay's father was quite wealthy, I understand."

"Hm. I suppose that's a possibility. But what if she *was* an illegitimate child? Why would Jay have hung onto an envelope about a cousin if that were the case? In a locked drawer, no less."

"You've got a point," said Alex. "Jay's attorney, Peter, could look into it, but you're talking about something that happened a long time ago, Julia."

"Yes, but if Melissa was a rightful heir when Jay's dad died, wouldn't she have been entitled to some of that estate?"

"Probably, but you're making a big leap in assuming that this Melissa exists and that she is a daughter of the senior Morrison."

"Let's assume for the moment that she exists and is his *daughter*, not a niece. What if she learned about Jay somehow and tracked him down and confronted him? And then killed him when he refused to acknowledge her or share his inheritance with her?"

Alex scoffed. "Sounds like a plot for a mystery novel to me."

Julia felt her hackles stiffen. "It could have happened. I'm not saying it did."

"It sounds pretty far-fetched. How would you go about proving it?"

Julia took a long swallow of her wine before answering. "I think the possibility should at least be considered. Nolan will want to listen to me. Or Detective Kilkelly."

"Are you serious?"

"It might be relevant information. Or not. I don't think I should make the decision myself about looking further into it."

"Your nephew will probably laugh about it."

"I'll take that chance, Alex. Thanks for your help. Good night." Julia looked at her phone and shook her head. She was conflicted about Alex's response. Surely he would want to know the truth as well. He was an attorney, after all. She resolved to call Nolan in the morning. She wanted to know what he learned from his chats with the golf buddies anyway, so it wouldn't be a wasted call.

JULIA REACHED Nolan mid-morning and told him what she and Carly had found the day before. He promised to swing by her office to pick up the copied records later in the day and discuss further investigation with Detective Kilkelly.

"Thank you, Nolan. I know it might be a red herring, but I appreciate your taking it seriously. Can you tell me if you learned anything from Jay's golf buddies?"

"Funny you should ask. One of them said Jay talked about this new distillery across the river in St. Jude. They had started producing some kind of grog. Jay told them he'd gotten a pint of it a couple of days earlier from one of his friends who had invested some seed money. His friend was having him taste it to see what he thought."

"What's the funny part?"

"There wasn't any kind of grog in Jay's liquor cabinet when I checked. Or in the garbage."

Julia felt her pulse quicken. "That could have been a good way to conceal the taste of methanol."

"Yeah. What kind of friend would have done that?"

"A former friend now, for sure. Do you think you can find out who that was?"

"We'll sure try. It might not be too hard."

JULIA FELT tired after the drive to and from Seattle the day before and had hoped to take a short nap during her lunch break. Instead, she made her way to the orthopedic unit to do a quick pre-op assessment of one of her partner's patients who needed a surgical procedure that afternoon. She had fallen at her residence the evening before and had fractured the humerus close to the shoulder joint. Fortunately for the patient it was her non-dominant arm.

She filled out the necessary forms after doing an examination, as well as talking with Mrs. Bisson's daughter and son-in-law at the bedside. While the elderly woman was not in the best of health, Julia's medical opinion was that she wasn't likely to have complications related to the necessary surgery, even urgently. Modern anesthesia and excellent orthopedic surgeons combined to create a high success rate for most patients, despite their risk profile.

Julia noticed LeAnne, the traveling nurse, waiting to accept the orders. Julia's eye caught the letter C behind her first name and a thought came to her. "What is your last name? I presume it starts with a C."

LeAnne glanced at her name tag before answering. "It's Carlton. Why?"

"You mentioned that your mother lived in Seattle. Is her name Gloria, by any chance?"

LeAnne's face paled. "Why do you ask?" Her hands shook as she signed off on Julia's order.

"Is your first name Melissa?" Julia cocked her head.

"Let me give these orders to the unit secretary and we can talk in the med room."

A few minutes later, Julia told LeAnne what she had discovered the day before and the background as to why she had been interested in her name. LeAnne admitted that her birth name was Melissa but that she had been called LeAnne by her mother since childhood. She'd never understood why.

She had finally learned about her real father about four

years earlier, when mysterious monthly bank deposits to her mother had stopped. Her mother subsequently learned he had died and told LeAnne the rest of the story, or at least some of it.

"I practically beat it out of her before she finally told me about how she'd met him and fallen in love without knowing he was already married and had a child. A boy." She blew her nose. "Mom was adamant against having an abortion and moved to Seattle to get away from him. He loved her too, I guess, and wanted to be sure she had enough money to raise me."

"A true love child," said Julia. "I wonder why he didn't try to get in touch with you or your mother once his other child was grown and gone."

"He did try a few times early on, Mom said, but she changed her phone number and tried to put the affair behind her. I wish I'd had the opportunity to know about him while he was alive."

"That must have been tough for her, and for you. Did you wonder about your father?"

LeAnne nodded, a somber smile on her face. "Of course. I wanted to have a daddy like my friends, but my mom was quite stubborn. And Catholic. I'm sure she was punishing herself in a way for her behavior. I don't think she realized I was being punished as well, being deprived of the opportunity to know a father. Anyway, after she learned he had died, she showed me his will. He'd sent her a copy years earlier. I was surprised I was listed as an heir. According to what I read in the media, he and his wife only had one child. And it wasn't me."

"So Jay Morrison was no longer an only child. That must have been a surprise to him when he found out."

"Yeah, I guess. It took a while to find him. Mom told me he had grown up on the other side of Lake Washington in Bellevue. I discovered that he went to college on the East Coast. Yale. So had his, I mean, *our* dad, it turns out. He stayed east and worked there for quite a few years before he ended up in Parkview, where he decided to start a bank with his father's— our father's—money."

Julia cocked her head. "Is that why you took this position? To be close to Jay?"

LeAnne laughed. "Pretty obvious, huh?" She shrugged. "I wanted him to know I existed and to talk with him about my share of the estate. I told him about the will my mother had, but he just laughed and told me to hire a really good attorney."

"How long ago did you talk with him? Was it recently?"

"No, no. I called him at least six months ago at the bank when I first learned he was here. I never got the chance to talk with him face-to-face before he died. I wish I had."

"This certainly makes things complicated. You understand that the detectives are going to want to talk with you, of course." Julia pictured LeAnne in the traditional orange jumpsuit worn by inmates at the county jail. *Had LeAnne met Jay after all, despite her denial? Was she the mystery guest at Jay's house?*

"Detectives? Why?"

"Jay was murdered. Didn't you know that?"

"I don't get the local paper and haven't heard any hubbub, not being a local myself."

"It hasn't been in the paper officially. May I tell the detective on the case how to contact you? They'll need to hear your story."

LeAnne nodded slowly with a thin smile as she wrote her cell number on the business card that Julia provided. "I didn't kill him. I never got to meet him."

CHAPTER 9
ESTATES AND PROBATES

Julia had a serious headache by the time she fixed herself dinner. She blamed missing lunch, punctuated by LeAnne's revelation. She hoped a double dose of caffeine in the form of a homemade cappuccino plus a couple of ibuprofens would work quickly. She knew she should call Alex to apologize for her being abrupt the evening before, but she realized she would also be gloating that her efforts of going through those files had paid off so decided against it.

She was halfway through the most recent episode of *Grey's Anatomy*, which she recorded faithfully for viewing when she had time, when Sophia's name popped up on her phone as it rang. "Hi. How are you holding up?"

"I could be better," said Sophia. "I've been nauseated the last several mornings and couldn't figure out what it was. I thought it was all the stress of the last week."

"And?"

"I talked with my best friend back home. She suggested I do a pregnancy test. I'm not sure what to do now."

Julia sat up straight. "You're pregnant?"

"It looks that way. The timing is right. Jay and I spent a weekend in Carmel exactly six weeks ago."

"This could complicate things."

"Don't I know it! Julia, should I talk to someone?"

"Probably. Let me run this by Alex and see what he thinks. I'll call you after I've tracked him down."

JULIA SIPPED on her now-lukewarm cappuccino while watching the rest of *Grey's Anatomy*. She envied the ease with which the television doctors solved complicated medical problems within an hour week after week. It didn't work as smoothly in real life. Nor did her detective work. She had found it helpful when in Amsterdam and Paris to discuss her mysteries with her sister, so she picked up the phone and called Carly. She didn't feel like talking to Alex just yet.

"Hey. Would you believe me if I told you I found Melissa?"

"No way," said Carly. "Not *that* fast. So who is she?"

"Turns out I had already met her but had no clue until I saw her name tag today at the hospital." Julia explained how she had figured it out.

"Wouldn't she have some claim to Jay's estate, like the money he inherited from his parents?"

"I wondered about that. I'll ask Alex when I call him in a bit. She'll certainly need a good attorney. And I can see how she might be considered a suspect in Jay's murder."

"I thought you had enough suspects already," said Carly.

"We need to add one more, or maybe I should say two more."

"Huh? I'm not following you."

"Sophia just called. She's pregnant."

"That could complicate things. But she's already on the list, so it's really only one more, if you want to be technical."

"Well, considering that the baby can't be a suspect, she would now have more motive than she did before."

"But she didn't know she was pregnant until after Jay was killed," said Carly. "Right?"

"Yep. At least that's what she says." Julia sat up quickly, startling Trixie, who had been sleeping at her feet. "Wait a minute. She mentioned not feeling well when I took her home after the gala. Do you suppose she did a pregnancy test before today? Like before Jay died?"

"But if she knew she was pregnant, it seems she would want him alive, not dead."

"You would think so. Now she's going to want to contest that will—if there really is a baby involved."

"When's the reading? It should be coming up soon."

"Tomorrow, is what I understand. I'm not sure who gets to be there. No matter what, Melissa—aka LeAnne—and Sophia will be contesting it. Jay's estate will have to go to probate."

Carly groaned. "I foresee a big mess."

"And we still don't know who the murderer is."

"You realize that's not your problem, don't you?"

"I feel responsible because of Sophia."

"Who's *also* not your problem."

"You're really a spoilsport sometimes, you know that?" Carly laughed.

Julia inhaled sharply. "I just thought of something. What about Jay's father's will? LeAnne said her mother showed her the will and she was named as an heir. How did Jay explain that away?"

"You should talk with Nolan. It's not your problem."

"You know I hate to abandon a good mystery."

"And you don't seem to mind almost getting killed either."

Julia sighed. Her sister had a point. "I know I owe you for finding me last spring in Paris, but *I* had to rescue *you* in

Amsterdam," said Julia. "Besides, this is Parkview. I'm not going to run into murderous art thieves or guys who want to steal sophisticated software."

"You seem to forget that there is at least one murderer out there, sis."

"Yeah, yeah, yeah. Okay. I'll talk to Nolan."

"Thank you. I'd like you to stay alive."

"Maybe *he'll* listen to my idea and let me help."

"Julia!"

JULIA ENJOYED TEASING her younger sister. Carly's honey-gold hair and sunny personality were a magical pheromone combination. Julia sometimes felt like one of Cinderella's wicked stepsisters when her sister was in the limelight. She had to be content with being a couple of inches taller plus having her father's dimples that Carly didn't have. She poured herself a glass of wine and settled back in her chair to call Nolan.

"Hi Nolan. Got a minute?"

"Sure. We just got the baby down for the night so I can relax for a while. What's on your mind?"

"I told you about finding the letter in those files in Seattle and wondering how we—I mean, you—would ever find Melissa," said Julia.

"I haven't even started that search. It's going to be like following a trail of old breadcrumbs."

"I know who she is."

"You do? How?"

Julia told her nephew about the traveling nurse who turned out to be Melissa LeAnne and shared her phone number. "I seriously doubt that she's your murderer, but it looks like she might have a vested interest in Jay's death."

"That's certainly true. I'll discuss this new information

with Detective Kilkelly. He'll want to investigate her recent movements. She would definitely qualify as a suspect despite how you feel about her. Money is a powerful motive."

"Do you want me to ask her to get you a copy of that will?"

"Sure, if she's willing. That would save some searching on my end."

"Will you be able to find out if it was ever sent for probate?"

"That will take longer, but I would think so. I'll probably have to check with our legal guys. Do you have anything more?"

"Only another potential heir to Jay's estate."

"Spit it out, Aunt Julia."

"Jay's girlfriend, Sophia, called me earlier and told me she's pregnant."

"Oh, boy. That's going to muddy the waters."

"It'll guarantee that Jay's will goes to probate."

"That too."

"One more thing—do you know if the will is going to be read tomorrow for sure?"

"That's what I understand from Kilkelly. Why?"

"I've read that gathering for will readings is no longer customary so I'm wondering why it's being done for Jay's will."

"It's because of the murder investigation. The detective wants to know who all the beneficiaries are in case there's someone else he must consider as a potential suspect. He requested that Peter call the meeting and has asked that the ex-Mrs. Morrison be there in addition to Kilkelly, the executor, Alex Gibson, and me."

Julia choked on her wine. "Alex is the executor?"

"Yes. You mean he didn't tell you?"

"He certainly didn't. I wonder why. Okay, last thing. Sophia told me she was supposed to stay in town until the will was read. Is she going to be there?"

"I don't think so, Aunt Julia. If she wasn't listed in the will, the attorney wouldn't have requested her. I understand that Kilkelly wanted her to stay here long enough to do the preliminary investigation but plans to let her leave tomorrow."

"Will her being pregnant change anything as far as being able to leave?"

"She'll obviously want to file a claim, but then she'll have to wait till the baby is born to prove paternity and all that."

"Of course."

"Is that all? I hear Maggie calling me to help with something in the kitchen."

"That's it. Thanks, Nolan. I'll see if I can get that copy of Mr. Morrison's will for you."

JULIA GROANED as she called Alex. She wondered why he hadn't told her he was Jay's executor, and wasn't sure she should ask.

"Are we going to play twenty questions again tonight?" he asked when he answered.

"No. I'm sorry I was such a goose last night. I'll blame it on that ugly drive home."

"You're forgiven. I was not at my best either. Are you feeling better tonight?"

"The headache I had earlier is gone, helped with caffeine and ibuprofen, but now I have a different problem."

"Is it something I can help with?"

"I hope so. What if I told you I found the mysterious Melissa?"

Alex whistled. "I'd say you should be a *real* detective. How did you do that?"

Julia explained how she'd put two and two together when

she noted LeAnne's name tag. "Could she still make a legal claim on her father's estate?"

"She'll need a top-notch attorney, but it can be done. I would also think she could find herself on the suspect list."

"I don't think she did it, Alex," said Julia. "She seems too nice."

Alex scoffed. "That's what people have said about a lot of bad guys."

"There's something else. Sophia's discovered she's pregnant. Would she have a claim on Jay's estate?"

"You probably know the answer is yes with a caveat or two."

"She'd like to talk to an attorney. Would you be willing to guide her?"

Julia heard a long sigh in the background.

"I wouldn't be able to represent her, being as my partner is Jay's attorney, but I could advise her on Washington state law."

"Would that be a potential conflict with you being Jay's executor?" Julia tried to keep her voice neutral despite feeling hurt that he hadn't told her.

"I'll stick to advising her on Washington state law. No conflict there," he replied, an icy edge to his voice.

"I'll let her know. Thanks, Alex. I appreciate it."

JULIA READIED for work more quickly than usual after her morning run with Trixie. She wanted to pop up to the orthopedic unit before seeing her own inpatients. She hoped to run into LeAnne to ask her about attending the reading of the will.

"I'm sure you're not surprised that I haven't received notification about a will reading," said LeAnne as she washed her hands after exiting a patient's room. "I wouldn't be able to attend anyway, with today's busy schedule. There are five total hips, two knee replacements, and a shoulder replacement on the schedule. That's a slug of post-op assessments and initial rehab sessions for one day." She smiled at Julia as she dried her hands. "And you and I both know I won't be named in the will."

"I won't be able to attend, either, but another friend of mine will let me know if there's anything unusual. And I'll share with you."

"Thanks. I'd appreciate that."

"As long as we're on the topic of wills, how long have you known about your father's will?"

"Only since he died. My mom didn't want to talk about it at all. Why?"

Julia walked with LeAnne to the nurse's station. "The deputy sheriff who's working on the case would like to have a copy of whatever you have. Would that be all right with you?"

"I guess so. I can bring it in with me tomorrow. Will that be soon enough?"

"That'll be fine. I'll come here about seven thirty tomorrow morning like I did today. Will that work?"

"Sure," said LeAnne. "I appreciate having you on my side. I've been so alone with this for such a long time."

Julia nodded slowly, not sure if she was truly on anyone's side. Sophia was an actress, after all, and LeAnne had done some conniving of her own. There was still the question of how Jay had claimed the entire estate when LeAnne was alive and well. Assuming this was the real LeAnne.

She shook her head as she trekked down the five floors and walked to her office two blocks away. She would help Nolan as much as he asked until the murderer was identified.

. . .

THROUGHOUT THE MORNING Julia found herself thinking about will probates whenever she had a minute between dictating charts or meeting with her patients. She didn't know the laws governing them, but knew that her attorney cousin would answer her questions even though that wasn't his area of expertise. Her morning clinic seemed to go more slowly than usual even though her mind was racing. She sent a text message to Nolan letting him know she would have a copy of Jay's father's will the next morning.

She used her lunch hour to do online research about wills and probates. A slew of conditions governed whether or not a specific will had to go to probate. At the end she knew a lot more about wills and probate but not the one thing she wanted to know: Did Jay's father's will meet the conditions that require probate? Even her cousin wouldn't be able to answer the answer without seeing the will itself. He would probably also need other details.

Afternoon clinic sped by. Julia picked up a roasted chicken and fresh green beans at the grocery store on her way home. Trixie wolfed down the leftovers from the quick meal. Julia liked to assume that it was a healthier meal overall than other fast-food options. Even if she followed it with an occasional splurge of Moose Tracks ice cream topped with Baileys Irish Creme liqueur. It was a favorite indulgence.

She curled up in her favorite chair, feet tucked under her, and pondered the facts of Jay's death as she knew them. Greg Lantz's wife's comments about offshore banking came to mind. Surely Alex would know something about that, she thought. And if he didn't know already, he might want to suggest a look into the bank's records, being that he was on the River City Bank's board of directors. Julia smiled to herself and counted to three in her head before she pressed the call button. Alex answered before she heard the first ring.

"You only get three questions tonight, Julia," he said. "My brain is very tired after today."

"I'm sorry about that. I wish I could help," she said softly. "I only have one question for you. I'm asking because Greg's wife made a comment about offshore banking accounts at the gala. I overheard her talk in the ladies' room. Do you know if Jay's bank was dabbling in that kind of account?"

"That's news to me. Do you know anything more?"

"No. Sorry. I didn't hear anything else. I trust you'll look into it?"

"You bet I will. You understand, don't you, that offshore banking by itself isn't illegal. Right?"

"I know nothing about it," said Julia. "It's one of those terms that tickles the imagination. Like Swiss bank accounts. I associate both of those with wanting to hide money."

Alex groaned. "Unfortunately, much of the time that's exactly why those accounts exist. You realize, of course, that the board doesn't get involved in the bank's operations or day-to-day management. The best I can do is bring it up at our next board meeting. Senior management always attends the open part of our sessions to answer questions that might come up. Like this one."

"Of course. Another topic. Can you tell me anything about Jay's will from today?"

"Nothing surprising, I suppose. Much of the money goes into a trust for his two sons. There's some for the theatre restoration, and some for Sophia and her acting enterprise."

"Oh! Was Sophia there? She told me she didn't expect to be named in the will."

"Peter called her this morning and invited her to attend. Jay had made changes very recently because of his divorce. He was already dating Sophia. Maybe she hit the jackpot."

"Did she bring up her pregnancy today?"

"Not that I know of, although she might have told Peter when he called her. That might be the *real* jackpot."

"Any mention of the half-sister?"

"No, and that's at least four questions, Julia."

"Sorry. I'm getting a copy of Jay's father's will tomorrow or the next day from LeAnne—I mean Melissa, who goes by LeAnne. She plans to make a formal request for probate."

"Do you have any happy news for me tonight?"

"Uh, no. Unless the fact that I haven't found any more new suspects counts as happy news." Julia raised an eyebrow even though Alex couldn't see it.

"Funny—not," said Alex. "Tomorrow's your day out of the office. Do you have any plans?"

"Not yet, which is unusual. But I'll come up with something. I'll have to let you know later. Are we on for dinner?"

"I'm going to have to cancel this time. I have some work that needs to get done."

Julia stopped tapping her foot. "I thought you were coming over for the dinner I owe you. Work can't wait?"

Alex sighed. "Not this time. I'm really sorry. How about we touch base Friday and talk about something for the weekend?"

"Sure. That's fine. One more question."

"Julia..."

"When's Jay's funeral?"

"Peter told me there wouldn't be one. Becca didn't want to make a public affair out of it. He didn't have any other living relatives as far as she knew so it would have been her and the boys and bank people. She had him cremated after the autopsy and that's that."

"That seems heartless."

"Some people will think so, but it's also less painful for Jay's sons."

"That's probably true."

"And that was at least five questions. Good night, Julia."

Julia sipped her wine as she mulled over Alex's unusual dinner cancellation. She was adult enough to not take it personally and accepted it as a gift of time. She now had a free evening in addition to her not-yet-decided plans for the day. Other than meeting LeAnne at the hospital before morning rounds, she decided to make use of the day for serious sleuthing.

CHAPTER 10
WILLED TO DEATH

Julia hurried through her morning routine to meet LeAnne on the ortho floor. "Any luck getting the will?"

"Hi, Dr. Julia. My mom is thrilled that you're willing to pursue this. She didn't know where to turn," LeAnne said as she produced a document from a zippered file folder. "Mom took it to her bank. They scanned it and emailed it to me. Do you really think you'll be able to recover my inheritance?"

"I know a good attorney who can look into this for you." Julia thumbed through the pages briefly before putting them back in the folder. "There's a lot to go through here, but he'll know what can be done."

"I've marked the pages where you'll find my name. I figured that would save you some time."

"Perfect. One more question. Do you know if this will went to probate?"

"Not sure, but if it did my mom and I weren't notified. Only way we knew my father had died was when the automatic bank deposits stopped suddenly about four years ago." LeAnne looked up from her work. "Why? Does that matter?"

"I did some online research and learned that wills are not necessarily made public unless they go to probate. It's possible that Mr. Morrison executed another document which would have invalidated this one."

"I hadn't thought of that. How will you find out?"

"I'll ask my lawyer friend how to go about it."

"It's never easy, is it? Thank you for doing whatever you can. I'll let my mom know."

LATER THAT MORNING Julia made herself comfortable in her den with a mug of her favorite peppermint tea and started a fire in the stone fireplace before logging onto her laptop. She presumed that Jay's father's will would have been filed and probated in King County. It wasn't as easy to find as she had hoped it would be. An hour later after searching through multiple webpages, she decided to call her cousin, Drew. She was still annoyed with Alex and didn't want to ask him any new questions related to LeAnne and her father's will.

Drew was a prosecuting attorney who worked in the King County prosecutor's office. He had said when he was younger that he'd rather put the bad guys in jail than defend someone for a crime, especially if there was proof that he or she was guilty. She hoped he would point her in the correct direction or maybe even find the documents for her if they existed. Normally she hesitated to use her Doctor title when trying to get through to someone on the phone, but it proved helpful today and she was connected with her cousin in short order.

"Hey, so nice to hear from you between the annual Christmas letters. My secretary said you had a question about a will. I'll help if I can. That's not my usual area of practice."

Julia gave him a thumbnail history of the will in question. Drew asked for pertinent details—name, approximate age and year of death. Within a couple of minutes of searching online he had found the documentation. Yes, the will had gone to probate in King County.

"This document says that the deceased's wife had died five years earlier, so the entire estate, other than a few bequests to a handful of charities, went to his son, William John Morrison, Jr."

"Are you sure? There's a half-sister who has a copy of a will that was executed in 1995 that names her as a co-beneficiary. Her name is Melissa LeAnne Carlton."

"Let me read more of this." Drew whistled a song from *Lion King* as she waited. "This will *had* been executed in 1995 so it's almost certainly the same one. Ah. There's a death certificate for a Melissa LeAnne Carlton that was produced at the time of the probate hearing. This says there were multiple attempts to locate 'said heir' but subsequent investigation found that she had died sometime prior to her father's death."

"What if I told you Melissa LeAnne is very much alive? Would she have any recourse to have the original will honored?"

"It's obviously too late for that, but she would very likely have a legitimate claim to proceeds from her half-brother's estate."

"That's what I hoped you would say. Can you recommend a good attorney for her? Her mom still lives in Seattle so I think that would be convenient."

"I'll send you a couple of names along with this document, which I presume you would like to see for yourself."

"Oh, yes." Julia gave him the details for emailing to her personal account. "Thank you, Drew. Let me know if I owe you anything for this. LeAnne is going to be thrilled when I tell her what you said."

"My pleasure. You can buy me dinner next time you're up this way."

Julia did a happy dance and squealed at the news. Trixie lifted her head to see what was going on but buried herself deeper into her bed after Julia scratched her behind the ears and kissed her on the nose. Julia walked back and forth across the room for a couple of minutes. Helping LeAnne to be able to claim her rightful share of her father's estate still didn't help identify the murderer. Julia refused to believe that LeAnne was capable of that kind of malice, especially when there were several other perfectly good suspects that needed to be fully vetted. She wondered if Alex had followed up on the comment Greg Lantz's wife had made at the gala.

"Sorry to call you at work but I can't stop thinking about Greg and those offshore accounts. Do you have a minute?"

"No problem," said Alex. "I was studying up on probate law and was ready to be done, anyway. And I'm sorry I was grumpy with you. This situation with Jay has everyone in our office upset and I let it get to me."

"Apology accepted. I had my talons out, too."

"What's on your mind?"

"Are there legitimate reasons that Greg and Jay would be using offshore accounts? Other than hiding money, I mean."

"Hm. Good question. I remember hearing that the CEO or CFO of one of the credit unions was buying short-term certificates of deposit somewhere in the Caribbean because he got a nice rate of return when interest rates were very low in the States. But that was at least fifteen years ago. I don't think that kind of investment would be sanctioned these days."

"Interest rates have been low for the past two years again. Maybe he was tempted to repeat history. Have you asked the bank auditors about any such activity at Jay's bank? Greg had to have been referring to *something*. Especially since his wife and Becca Morrison were the ones talking about it."

"You're right. I suppose I can make a couple of calls and ask questions before the next board of directors meeting. I hope it turns out to be nothing more than talk, or there could be some interesting headlines."

"Thanks, Alex. I owe you for this."

"I'll accept one of your home-cooked meals. Deal?"

Julia laughed. "Deal."

Julia checked for an email from Drew but found nothing yet. She hopped up from her chair and wandered out to her deck in the backyard. She admired the maple leaves colored in rich reds and golds still clinging to the trees as though they could avoid the inevitable fall to the ground. The next brisk wind would surely blow most of them off and onto the lawn where they would collect until Julia's yardman came on his biweekly schedule. While she loved to plant her flowers and enjoyed pruning her many shrubs, Julia loathed the job of mowing and edging. And blowing leaves. She was glad to pay her gardener for those tasks.

She watched one of the ubiquitous gray squirrels thoroughly check an acorn before popping it in his cheek and scampering up the tree to its nest. It triggered a thought she'd had while at Jay's house. She had noticed multiple containers of hand sanitizer in his home. He'd had a couple of them in the dining room, on the kitchen counter and table, and even in his bedroom. It seemed excessive considering he lived alone and didn't have small children in the house. It reminded her of Jack Nicholson's character in *As Good as It Gets*. He'd had an extreme case of obsessive-compulsive disorder. Julia made a mental note to ask Sophia about it.

Twenty minutes passed by and there was still no email

from Drew. Unable to focus on anything else, Julia sat down and jotted down a list of questions that nagged at her brain about Jay. Where was his laptop? Was there something on it that caused it to be stolen? Or was he keeping something on it secret? Why did he have a .357 Magnum? Where were those missing ESCO and Melissa files? What was the story about the offshore accounts? Who produced the death certificate at his father's probate? What did he do when he lived back East? Who shot at Drake and why? Did Jay know he had a heart condition? Did he know that his father had it? Had Jay ever told Becca about his half-sister? Who had a drink with him Friday night and what did they drink? And did anyone else know about it?

Julia flinched when her laptop pinged the arrival of an email. She opened it immediately when she saw that it was from Drew. He had attached several files including the will itself which, on first glance, appeared to be the same as the one LeAnne had shared with her. The largest file was the legal judgment itself which boiled down to Jay's entitlement to the entire estate after a few bequests were honored. Julia didn't see a mention anywhere of the value of William Morrison's estate but surmised that it was much larger than her own retirement account based on the size of his bequests, each of which was six figures.

The third attachment was very short. A letter from a law firm in Hartford, Connecticut, stipulated that the heir named as Melissa LeAnne Carlton had died as of two years prior to Mr. Morrison's death. A photocopied death certificate had been attached to the original document to support the claim. Julia felt her heart thud.

CHAPTER II

FISHING EXPEDITION

"Hi, Nolan. I just received a copy of Jay Morrison's father's probated will and there's something interesting that you'll want to check out. According to a letter that was submitted for the probate proceedings, Melissa LeAnne Carlton had been declared dead."

"That *is* news. Are you in the office today? I can come by and pick it up if that's okay with you."

"Come by the house. I'll be here for the next hour or so."

Julia curled up in her grandma's chair in her den. How could she learn more about the world of Jay Morrison before he showed up in Parkview? Would Sophia know anything? Did she dare call Becca, who would know his history, seeing as how she was part of it? Choosing certainty over doubt, she called Becca, who Julia assumed would be staying in Parkview at least till the end of the current school term which ended just before Christmas.

"Uh, hi, Julia," said Becca. "I must say I'm surprised to hear from you. What is this I hear about you helping the police in the investigation of Jay's death?"

"Technically I'm helping Nolan, but only unofficially. It bugs me when I can't make sense out of what appear to be facts."

"I'm not following you. What are you talking about?"

"I'm sure you've been told that Jay died from his kidneys shutting down apparently due to methanol poisoning."

"Yes, and..."

"The deputy sheriff and police detective have not been able to find a source of methanol anywhere at the house. I was wondering if he used it in his garage or a workshop, perhaps?"

Becca scoffed. "Jay detested getting his hands dirty or doing any kind of mechanical work or labor. He hired someone to mow the lawn for that reason, among others. You obviously haven't seen his garage or you would have noticed that it's pristine and he had no tools of any kind."

"That's good to know. I have another question. I've heard that you and Jay moved to Parkview from somewhere on the East Coast and that Jay worked in real estate before he started the bank. Is that correct?"

"I'm not sure if you could call it real estate. We lived near Hartford, Connecticut. He worked for a company that developed shopping malls and other large complexes. He was responsible for making the deals with the companies that moved into them."

"Do you mean the outlet shopping centers?"

"Yes, exactly, although his company wasn't one of the biggest developers. The name was something like Globisphere, or maybe Global Sphere. I couldn't keep the official name straight. They were based in Hartford, I know for sure. Anyway, Jay was working his way up the management ladder and was about to take charge of a new project in Ohio, but then his father died and left him a lot of money. That's when he decided to get out of that business and start his own bank."

"Why did he choose Parkview?"

"He did some research into banking laws and got some advice from his attorney friends. One of them told him about an opportunity here and helped him get started."

"Who was that? Do you remember?"

"Of course. It's Peter Lewis, his attorney here in town."

Julia promised to keep Becca informed about the methanol poisoning issue. While she believed that Becca was most likely innocent in Jay's death, there was still a possibility that she was involved. Factors against that idea were that she was the other-parent guardian of Jay's sons and would have reasonable access to funds, it seemed, and also had a nice settlement from the divorce. Or so rumor had it. Julia found herself wondering about the liquidity of Jay's assets. What if he had tied up most of his money in non-liquid assets? Becca might not have easy access after all. She slapped her hand on her desk when she realized she should have asked about the offshore accounts comment at the gala. Maybe Jay's assets were tied up there. She made a mental note to ask Becca at the next opportunity.

Trixie jumped up from her cozy dog bed and ran to the front door when the doorbell rang. She had learned that one ding meant someone was at the side door and that ding-dong was the front door alert. Julia followed and greeted Nolan.

"Hey. Thanks for coming by. Saves me a trip to the sheriff's office." Julia scooped up the extra copy of the will that she'd printed out and shuffled through the pages to the death certificate, which she handed to Nolan. "Take a look at this. It can't be real, considering that I know Melissa LeAnne in person."

Nolan perused the document. "It looks authentic to me but forgers are very good these days. It says she died in 2014. That would have been about two years before the senior Mr. Morrison." He thumbed through the rest of the file. "I'll have this checked out."

"Have you found Jay's laptop yet?"

"Not a trace. We checked his office at the bank and interviewed his managers and secretary. They all said the same thing—that he never brought it to work. It stayed at his house as far as they all knew. One of the managers said she wasn't sure he actually owned one because he was so secretive about it."

"It's gotta be somewhere." Julia stood near the dining table, her fingers drumming the surface. "Would Becca have it? But how and when would she have gotten it from Jay?"

Nolan chuckled at his aunt's playing detective. "Going back to the death certificate—what if the woman you know as LeAnne is an imposter? Maybe the real Melissa LeAnne *is* dead and the mother found someone to pose as her daughter to claim the inheritance. Is that possible?"

Julia nodded her head up and down slowly with furrowed eyebrows. "It's certainly a possibility that I hadn't considered. But DNA testing would prove that one way or another and they wouldn't get away with it for long. Although his body was cremated." She looked at Nolan. "Do you know if his DNA was saved, perhaps from the hospital?"

Nolan shook his head. "That's a good question. I hope so." His cell phone chirped as if on cue. "Gotta get going, Aunt Julia. I'll follow up on this death certificate and let you know. Maggie says to tell you hi of course." He pecked her on the cheek and left, cell phone to his ear.

Julia remembered a few minutes later that she had forgotten to ask him about Drake's shooting incident.

PAM WAS DELIGHTED that Julia had offered to pick her up at work and take her to lunch at a new cafe near Julia's office. A couple of graduates from a well-known culinary school in Portland had talked the management of a credit union into letting them open a small restaurant on the premises of its new business center. The Metro Grill was open for breakfast and lunch and promised quick service for people with limited lunch time. It had proven successful so far, with five-star reviews online both for the quality of the food and prompt service.

"I don't get off the mill site for lunch very often so this is a real treat," Pam said as they studied the menu.

After their food orders were taken by a young waitress wearing a crisp white shirt and black pants, Pam said, "You asked about Drake and the potshot at his house."

"Has anything turned up in the investigation?"

"I don't think so but Drake has been acting strangely since that happened."

"Strange in what way?"

The waitress, Danielle, delivered their beverages. Julia sipped her raspberry Italian soda and smiled. "This is yummy."

Pam taste-tested her cappuccino. "So is this. Let's see if I can explain what I mean. He's been edgy, and almost paranoid about work. For example, he doesn't want to go out for dinner in case someone sees him and wants to ask about the bank."

"That doesn't seem unusual to me. I don't like being asked about work when I'm out to dinner."

Pam shook her head. "This is different. Drake normally loves to talk about the bank and about making money and investments. It's his world." She made air quotes with her fingers.

"Does he think someone shot at him because they're mad at the bank?"

"He thinks someone in the union is trying to make his life miserable since Jay took over the major part of the ESCO account. Adam Johns believes Drake lost most of the missing money at Parkview National before the account was transferred to River City."

Julia smiled at Danielle, who hovered at the table with their sandwich and chips already divided in two portions for them to share. "Thank you, young lady. It looks delicious." Julia bit into the hefty BLT. "This is great. Where do restaurants find juicy, ripe tomatoes at this time of year?" Julia wiped the errant juice off her chin. "Can you tell me more about the ESCO mess?"

"I know more about it from hearing the talk at the mill than from Drake, which I suppose is expected. Drake shouldn't be sharing sensitive information with me, anyway."

"I take that comment to mean that he does share sometimes."

Pam shrugged a shoulder. "Guys talk. Anyway, he handled that pension account personally."

"Suggesting that he's taking the loss of that money personally as well."

"Exactly."

Julia munched on some chips. "I overheard Becca Morrison and Sandy Lantz mention offshore accounts at the gala. It sounded like Greg had stumbled onto something he wasn't supposed to know about. I got the impression it had to do with the union, but I can't tell you why I thought that. Do you know anything?"

"That's interesting. I know they aren't illegal per se, but if they're used to hide money it's a different story."

"I mentioned it to Nolan earlier, but I'll ask if he ever asked Greg Lantz about that comment by his wife. Alex brushed me off when I mentioned it to him."

"Maybe it's a touchy subject?"

Julia nodded. "He's been acting a little strange lately as well. He cancelled out on me for dinner tonight. Said he had work to do." She looked at Pam. "Could they possibly be in on something together?"

CHAPTER 12
AND THE SUSPECTS ARE...

Julia was happy to learn that Sophia was still in town. She hadn't talked with her since prior to the reading of the will the day before. Although Sophia was planning to fly to San Francisco early the next morning, she was available to help Julia with some detective work before she left. They met at the town's public library where they commandeered a couple of available computers for their research.

"Thanks for helping me with this, Sophia. Alex mentioned that you were named in Jay's will after all. I'm guessing that was a surprise to you."

"Totally! Peter Lewis called me yesterday morning and said I could attend the reading, but I didn't want to face Becca. I wasn't feeling all that great anyway. He told me Jay had left me some money, which, as I told you a couple of days ago, I didn't expect."

"How nice! That should help with a baby on the way."

"It feels more like a consolation prize right now." She looked at Julia with somber eyes. "Okay, Julia. Let's get to work. Tell me what we're looking for."

"Right. Your assignment is to search for an outlet developer based in Hartford, Connecticut. Becca said it was called Globisphere or something to that effect. Then you're going to call and pretend to be doing a background check on a prospective employee."

Sophia smiled. "By the name of Jay Morrison? Clever."

"They may have him listed by his legal first name, William, instead of Jay."

"Then let's get started before everyone goes home in Connecticut. It's already a quarter after four there."

Sophia found the company, Globisphere, LTD, within a few minutes and hit pay dirt on her call. She bluffed her way through to the director of human resources, who gave her an answer which left the terms of Jay's departure vague. Sophia asked if she could talk to someone who had direct knowledge of his work. That person, Michael McDonald, was out of the office until the next day, Friday. Sophia promised to call again.

In the meantime, Julia reached out to the law firm that produced the death certificate for LeAnne. She knew Nolan was planning to follow up on that, but he was checking with the State of Washington's database. Julia wanted to know how the attorney obtained it for the probate hearing. She figured it wasn't privileged information if the person in question was dead. She reached the right office without difficulty but discovered that they required authorization to release any information, even for a dead person. By the time she talked to Nolan and gave him the details for faxing the authorization, it was after office hours.

The two women dropped in at the Back Door Office and brooded over their cosmopolitans.

"It's so annoying to have to deal with the time difference between west and east coasts," said Julia.

"And what we find out may not be helpful in the end."

"I'm sure it will be helpful but not exactly in what way. What time tomorrow are you headed back to San Francisco?"

"My flight is at seven a.m. and it's only a couple of hours long. My agent said he talked to the film director who is going to let me do an audition next week. He thinks I'll get the part." Sophia smiled wistfully, finished her drink, and grabbed her coat. "I hung out here a couple of extra days in case Becca decided to have a funeral but that's not happening. When I get back home I'll have a pity party all by myself with a couple of friends who had met Jay."

"That's a nice idea, actually. No bad vibes in the air like there would be here." Julia hugged Sophia. "Be sure to let me know what you find out from Globisphere."

JULIA SAT down at her dining table with a legal pad and pen. Something about Jay's death still didn't make sense. She'd always found it helpful to put things on paper when the facts didn't put themselves together in a logical way. She started by making a list of the potential suspects and what they might gain from Jay's death.

Drake Ashford, as president of Parkview National Bank, wouldn't necessarily gain anything directly. His bank and its member-owners would benefit indirectly, perhaps, if there was a shift of bank accounts from River City to Parkview. There was also the issue of the union money and how it might look to the public. Julia had felt the tension between Drake and Jay at the gala. But was that a motive for murder?

Becca Morrison already had a divorce settlement and, as the guardian for Jay's young sons, had access to the rest of his money with his death. So why would she risk spending her life in jail and leaving her boys motherless? Julia made a note to find out about Becca's family and where she was from. East Coast, perhaps?

Adam Johns and the ESCO union members were unhappy with how they thought their money had been handled. But they were madder at Drake, weren't they? Why would they, or he, go after Jay?

Sophia Alder benefited more by having Jay alive. He had told her he would finance her career. If she knew he had included her in his will, maybe she had a motive, but otherwise she didn't. Until she turned up pregnant.

Greg Lantz was second-in-command at Jay's bank. Was he the Friday night visitor who had a drink with Jay? Did he taint it with methanol? Did he aspire to being the president and kill Jay as the most expedient way to gain the position? Sandy's comments implied that he was more of a figurehead and resented how he was treated by Jay. But murder?

Julia felt obligated to add LeAnne to the list, although she did so reluctantly. She had a motive—unless she *was* dead after all—and opportunity. Was she the person with whom Jay had had a drink, despite her claim that she'd never met him? And it was possible she knew how to poison someone with methanol, given her training as a nurse. She could have been seeking revenge for depriving her of her rightful inheritance, which would also have helped her support her mom as she aged.

LeAnne looked like the most likely suspect in her brief analysis, but Julia refused to believe she was capable. Nurses were trained to save lives, not take them.

Julia poured herself a glass of Capstone Cellars cabernet and curled up in her thinking chair. What else could have caused Jay's untimely death? Where did that methanol come from?

Julia suddenly sat up straight and reached for her laptop on the end table. She searched for an article she had read a few weeks back about tainted hand sanitizer. During the early weeks of a recent pandemic, there had been a run on all kinds of cleaning agents, especially hand sanitizers. Even now, though panic had subsided, containers of sanitizers were ubiquitous—they were stationed at the entrance to every store, restaurant, office, and even inside the church.

She found several references to hand sanitizers that had significant levels of methanol when tested. Becca had mentioned Jay's aversion to dirt and germs. Julia had noticed bottles of hand sanitizer in several rooms at Jay's home. Methanol can be absorbed through the skin. Was that the source of his poisoning? His underlying heart condition might have been inherited from his father or could have been caused by his drinking too much alcohol. Either way it could make his system vulnerable, leading Julia to surmise that he could have developed methanol poisoning from his incessant use of a contaminated product.

She called Nolan and shared her thoughts. He promised to have the hand sanitizers tested.

The bells at the nearby Catholic church chimed the hour. Four o'clock. LeAnne should be done with her day shift at the hospital. Julia wanted to know more about LeAnne—the real one or imposter—and took a chance by calling her.

"Hi. I didn't expect to hear from you so soon. Have you learned anything more about my dad's will?"

"Some. Can you meet me for happy hour? I'll tell you what I know."

THIRTY MINUTES later they sat in a cozy booth at Grant's at the Montpelier Hotel. The vintage wooden booths had come from an old hotel back east. They were set in a row of four with tall dark wood backs (Julia guessed they were mahogany or cherry) separating one from the other. They were completely enclosed on the top as well and had ornate carving on the front edges. They weren't soundproof but felt very private once seated inside.

With her favorite cabernet and LeAnne's chardonnay having been served, Julia shared what she and Nolan had discussed when she showed him the senior Mr. Morrison's will.

LeAnne sputtered on her wine when Julia mentioned the idea that Nolan thought she could be an imposter. Then she laughed. "Why would I even attempt that? DNA testing would disprove that fallacy. I swear I'm the real thing." She crossed her heart as in a childhood pledge. "I'll give you a sample right now if you like."

Julia pressed her lips together as she wondered if LeAnne had crossed the fingers of her other hand behind her back. "I believe you, LeAnne. I really do. The detectives will do their research into the death certificate. My cousin, Drew, an attorney in Seattle, told me that it's difficult, if not impossible, to undo the results of your father's probate decision, but you can file a challenge to Jay's will. That will force it to go to probate. Here's the list he sent me of attorneys in Seattle who can help you with that."

"Thank you. Is there anything else you can share with me? I haven't heard from the local detective lately."

Julia shared her thoughts on the likely suspects if Jay had been murdered and shared that she had asked Nolan to have the hand sanitizers checked for methanol. "Another question for you. Do you know if your father had any kind of medical conditions, like heart disease?"

"Neither my mom nor I have had any contact with him in years, so unless he told her something years ago, the answer would be no." She tilted her head. "What condition are you thinking of?"

"The autopsy showed that Jay had cardiomyopathy, which can be inherited but can also be caused by excessive alcohol use. A double whammy in Jay's case. Add some methanol and you have a formula for accidental death."

"Or purposeful if someone throws in the methanol with intent to kill."

Julia nodded thoughtfully at LeAnne's response. *Did LeAnne know something? Or nothing?* "That's the part I'm having trouble with."

"What do you mean?"

"It seems that no one knew about Jay's heart condition though his alcohol use was out in the open. Did someone have the knowledge to use methanol to hasten his demise? I still wonder if his Friday evening visitor doctored up a drink. I can't imagine him drinking the sanitizer."

LeAnne's face didn't flinch.

CHAPTER 13

MISSING PUZZLE PIECES

J ulia entered her house to the sound of the landline phone ringing. She hurried to answer it even though most of the calls were robocalls these days. She had a few older patients who still called her at home. She heard a "click" as she picked up the receiver. The caller ID was a local number but there wasn't a name attached. "Oh well, they'll call back if they want me," she said to Trixie, who was prancing up and down. "Let's go for a walk. Find your leash."

The brisk air called for gloves and a scarf to go with Julia's lightweight, puffy jacket. She breathed deeply as if to cleanse the bad spirits out of her lungs and clear her mind. The shorter half of Lake Sacajawea required thirty-five minutes of walking at a 3.8 miles-per-hour pace. Just enough to keep her in shape and give herself thinking time as well.

After feeding her dog and checking for mail, Julia started a fire in her den and curled up in her chair, feet tucked up in a blanket. "CRAAACK." She jumped up and ran into her dining room, nearly tripping on Trixie, who had jumped up from her bed and scrambled to the commotion as well. Broken glass littered the hardwood floor. She scooted Trixie away from the shards and heard a motorcycle speeding down the quiet street. She looked each way out the front door but didn't see anything unusual in either direction. Her heart raced wildly as she grabbed her phone and dialed Nolan.

For the first time ever, she wished she had one of those camera-lens doorbells which might have picked up the motorcycle as it slowed down and aimed at her house. Maybe a neighbor had a security camera. She shuddered as her adrenalin surged. She was livid that someone would deliberately damage someone else's property, but thankful she wasn't hurt. She paced the floor, phone in hand, waiting for the police.

Detective Kilkelly was at her door within seven minutes, having been alerted by Nolan, who showed up a few minutes later. They found a small-caliber bullet wedged in the wall opposite the window. Nolan nailed a piece of plywood over the single pane which had been broken. Julia was glad she had the old-fashioned windows with multiple panes. A larger window would have been much harder to clean up and cover over.

Julia and the officers took seats in her living room. She told them what had happened while they took notes.

"I would guess someone is unhappy with your poking around into Jay's death," said Nolan.

"That or a violent patient, which I doubt," said Julia.

"Have you talked to anyone that I don't know about?"

"I don't think so. At least not anyone who rides a motorcycle and shoots bullets into houses."

"Who *did* you talk to? Today, for starters," asked Kilkelly.

"I chatted with LeAnne Carlton this morning at the hospital, and later we met and had a drink. I talked to Becca Morrison on the phone late morning." Julia hugged herself as she chilled. "And I met Sophia at the library. We were looking up the company that Jay worked for in Hartford. Nothing dangerous, I promise."

"You've been busy, Aunt Julia. And I'm not sure you know what dangerous means."

"You may have triggered something that someone doesn't want us to find out," said Kilkelly. "We'll canvass the neighborhood for cameras and witnesses."

Nolan said, "That phone call may have been to find out if you were home."

Julia shivered. "I just thought of that, myself. Next time I'll let it go to the answering machine. Can you trace the call?"

"We'll try," said Kilkelly. "If it was a scammer, it'll be hard to trace back to the original number. And it takes time."

"One of us will touch base with you tomorrow. Keep your doors locked, Aunt Julia."

"I'll arrange for more frequent patrols of the neighborhood," said Kilkelly.

Julia managed a grim smile as the officers left. She locked the door and pulled the curtains closed as if they could protect her from harm. She shivered even though the house was warm and she was curled up in a blanket—an old quilt her mother had made—in her grandma's chair. She whispered a prayer of thanks to her guardian angels for her safety. She had almost gone into her dining room earlier to work on a jigsaw puzzle she'd started before the craziness of Jay's death. She was angry that her privacy had been violated and scared for the same reason. Ten minutes later she felt calmer and her heart had stopped racing but she didn't want to be alone. She considered calling Alex, but he'd said he would be busy and she was still miffed that he hadn't told her he was Jay's executor. Plus he'd seemed distant all week. It seemed he was holding back on something.

"Hey, Carly. Are you busy? Can I come out to your house for a while?"

JULIA PICKED up takeout fish and chips at Marv's Fish House on the way to her sister's home about twenty minutes away. Carly and Rob lived on ten acres of what had been part of the sisters' paternal grandparents' strawberry farm many years earlier. The property was high on a hill overlooking the Columbia River facing west. Sunsets were fabulous through the long summer, and on a clear evening the rest of the year. On this evening the chilly breeze prevented sitting outside. The sunset was long gone, anyway.

Carly and Julia sat in the cozy living room facing the darkening sky over the river, enjoying the meal with a glass of cabernet. Julia didn't ascribe to any rules of white meat or fish calling for white wine, at least not in the fall and winter, when she preferred red.

"You sounded distressed when you called," said Carly. "What's up, sis?"

"Someone shot a bullet into my house earlier."

"What? No!"

"Yeah. Scared Trixie and me half to death. I'm glad I don't have big, modern plate-glass windows in the front of the house. For once, I'm grateful for old-fashioned mullioned windows with their small panes."

"Less mess to clean up and less expensive to replace. I'm glad *you're* okay. Windows are easy to fix." Carly leaned over to put an arm around her sister. "Any idea who it was? It sounds like what happened to Drake."

"It does, doesn't it? Nolan and Detective Kilkelly think the same thing, of course. I heard what sounded like a motorcycle speeding away after I heard the glass break."

"And of course, nobody saw or heard anything."

"They're checking with the neighbors now but at this time of year people are inside their warm houses, not doing yard work in the front. Small chance of any witnesses. Maybe not any security cameras either. If there were, I think most of them would be covering the backyards, not the front side of the house."

"We have a doorbell camera. What about those?" Carly sipped her wine. "Thanks for bringing the wine with you. All I had to offer was a hard cider. Rob's preferred drink."

"I know. That's why I came prepared." She saluted her sister with her glass. "I'm afraid that in my neighborhood, a security doorbell camera would go off every time a car drives down the street or someone walks up the sidewalk. That would drive me crazy. Maybe a neighbor will install one."

"That's a thought. Tell me what you're thinking about Jay being murdered versus not murdered. It's been a while since you caught me up."

"That's why I'm here. I thought with our two heads together we might be able to figure out which direction to go to figure this out." Julia told Carly her current thoughts on the murder suspects and why none of them made any sense. "Then I started to think of Jay's death from another angle. What if he wasn't murdered, but died accidentally because of his obsessive use of hand sanitizer that happened to be contaminated by methanol?"

"I saw something about that on the news, myself. I'm guessing you told Nolan your theory and he's checking it out."

"Correct. Jay's still dead and there's still a problem with his half-sister showing up out of the blue. I like LeAnne but why did she wait? She's known about him for the last four or five years."

"I suppose it could have taken her this long to track him

123

down. It's not like her mother and biological father have kept in touch for the last thirty-five years."

"I find her timing incredibly interesting." Julia sat back in the big chair and tucked her feet under her. "I don't want her to be the guilty party but I can't entirely exclude her either."

A few minutes passed in silence. They watched a large container ship move slowly up the river toward Portland, where it would be unloaded only to be reloaded for the return trip back toward the Pacific Ocean, its final destination unknown. When Julia and her siblings were young they had learned to recognize the flags flying on the stern which identified the country of origin of the ship. Nowadays ships were often registered in another country.

Julia said, "Let's set murder suspects aside and think about the other unsolved parts of this. There's still the question of offshore accounts that Sandy Lantz mentioned."

"And you mentioned a .357 Magnum gun in Jay's file cabinet. Do you know if the detective has had it checked for having been used?"

"Nolan took it that first day, so I think so."

"The union funds trading issue is still up in the air according to what I get from Rob. The guys mention it from time to time in the union hall or lunchroom."

"And Jay's laptop is still missing."

"Like Pierre's in Paris. Maybe it'll have love letters inside," said Carly, daring a giggle.

"It's a laptop, not a briefcase, Carly."

"There could still be email letters from Sophia," she retorted.

"That reminds me. I got an email from Josh last week." Julia grinned at her sister. Her parting with Josh last spring in Paris had been difficult, to say the least. It was bad enough that Julia had gotten dangerously involved in a case when Josh's business colleague, Pierre, had turned out to be a killer. On top of that, Josh had invited her there for what she'd expected to be a romantic week. Only he'd taken up with someone else between the invitation and her trip, and he'd only admitted it at the end of that week. Julia had been grateful she'd enticed Carly to travel with her.

"I was afraid to ask if you'd heard anything from him. Was it a good email?"

"More or less. He's not dating that Retha person anymore. He said it was too complicated to explain."

"What else? You have a funny look on your face."

Julia felt her face redden. "His company is considering expanding to the West Coast. Josh might be coming this way to look at Portland or Seattle."

"And he wants to see you..."

"Something like that." Julia took a long swallow of her wine. "I won't get my hopes up, but I look forward to seeing him—if he actually makes the trip. And doesn't find someone else in the meantime."

Carly rolled her eyes. "Well, tell him I said hi when you write back."

"Of course. Now let's get back to Jay's laptop. He probably didn't have proprietary software like Pierre was trying to steal, but he could have had information related to ESCO union funds. There was an empty file folder labeled ESCO in his dining room when Sophia and I were there that first day."

"Good thought. Wasn't there also an empty Melissa folder? You mentioned that when we did the Seattle gig."

"Yes. Do you suppose he was copying the files into his laptop and destroying the originals? I found a couple of random bank statements for ESCO that I gave to Nolan and the detective. It just doesn't make sense trying to put these bits and pieces together."

Carly laughed. "Even though we're experts at putting 1,000-piece jigsaw puzzles together at the beach house."

"This puzzle has a couple of very important missing pieces."

"You'll find them, Julia. You always do."

CHAPTER 14

BROTHERHOOD CONNECTION?

Between patients on a busy Friday, Julia squeezed in a call to her nephew Nolan to ask for permission to talk with Drake about the ESCO account.

"What are you trying to find out?"

"I hope he can give me some help with the statements that I found at Jay's house, unless you've already had them scrutinized. I wonder if there's a discrepancy between what Drake's records show as the transfer amount going out from his bank and what it shows on Jay's incoming records."

"I think Detective Kilkelly would be okay with that. That shouldn't be violating anyone's rights."

"Thank you! I'll call Drake right away."

"There's one condition. You have to tell me what you find out. Sooner, not later."

"Yes, Nolan. I'll do that."

DRAKE WAS happy to meet Julia at her office during her lunch break. He brought several printouts for the account in question

—one at the opening of the account, one for each December, and the final statement at the time of transfer to Jay's bank. In all, he had ten statements representing the eight years the account had been at Parkview National.

Julia had two non-consecutive statements from Jay's bank. One was dated July the previous year, which was seven months after the account had been opened, and one was dated August of the current year. "According to these statements," she said, "Jay's bank had the union's pension money for almost two years."

"That's correct," said Drake. He studied the balances for a few moments, using his cellphone calculator to do the math. "It looks like there's a loss of about four hundred twenty-five thousand dollars since the transfer between Parkview National and River City banks and last August." He did a couple more calculations. "Most of that change occurred between July of last year and August this year. I can't tell any more than that without additional information from the account at River City."

"Wow. That's a lot of money. No wonder Adam Johns is unhappy. Do you recall if there was something big that happened in the stock market during that time to cause that big of a swing in the year between these two statements?" Julia had noticed the large difference herself. But she hadn't known the value of the account at the time of the transfer. She saw for herself that Drake was right: the big drop came after the transfer.

Drake nodded. "It looks like a lot of money disappeared from this account but there's no paper trail to tell me where it went." He spent another several minutes with the statements, shaking his head at the end. "Is this all you have?"

"It's everything that was left in the file at Jay's house. I'm sure Adam Johns from ESCO would have more information."

"I'll get in touch with him. There's definitely something suspicious going on here."

"Greg Lantz's wife mentioned offshore accounts to Becca at the gala. Do you suppose that's where the money went?"

"It's a possibility."

"I know nothing about high-level banking, Drake. How do those accounts work?"

"Typically, someone with money to spare, or maybe to hide, opens an account in a country that prevents the release of the identities of the owners of the account."

"Like in a foreign country?"

"Yes. We're all familiar with the term Swiss bank accounts, as an example. But the term originated from the Channel Islands being offshore from the United Kingdom. Most offshore banks are still located in island nations, but the term is now used to refer to any bank used for their advantages."

"Which advantages are those? Remember, I'm a novice at this."

Drake smiled. "Sorry. Most of the time, an individual or company will maintain an offshore account for financial and legal advantages. There's greater privacy, little or no taxation, easy access to deposits, and protection against local, political, or financial instability. That last point can be important in counties with civil unrest or shaky monetary systems. That's not a problem so much here in the U.S."

"Why would Jay have been using them, if he was, in fact, doing so?"

"Considering what I know of Jay's background, he may have had a large personal fortune that he wanted to protect, which isn't illegal."

"Unless he was hiding it from someone," said Julia.

"We don't know if he was hiding money, or if he *had*

offshore accounts for sure. Sandy's offhand comment could have been about something else."

"Maybe. But I don't think so." Julia shook her head.

"Okay. Enough on that. I heard you got shot at too. Are you making someone mad?" Drake let out a nervous chuckle.

"Same as you. Any ideas as to who this crazy person is?"

"No. The police told me they don't have any leads at all. They want to chalk it up to a random event but that's hard to do when there have been two similar incidents."

Julia heard Amie's gentle knock on the door a couple of seconds before her medical assistant poked her head in. "Thanks, Amie. We're just wrapping up."

Drake collected his papers and stood. "I gotta run too."

"Yeah. Well, thanks, Drake, for the lesson. I'll let you know if I learn anything new about any of this."

JULIA BARELY NOTICED the time during the afternoon and was surprised that it was almost six when she finished her clinic dictations for the day. She and Alex had settled into a routine of eating out on most Friday nights so she didn't have to do anything for dinner except be ready when he came by at about seven o'clock.

While Julia loved living in the Pacific Northwest overall, the one exception to that was the fact that from November to February it was dark in the morning when she left her house to make hospital rounds and again in the evening when she headed home. If she didn't leave the hospital during her lunch hour, she wouldn't see daylight all day because her office and exam rooms were windowless. And she rarely had time to make an escape because she used her lunch break time to do dictations and review the morning's lab and X-ray results.

The doctor's parking area in the four-story parking garage

was half-empty and darkly lit, which was typical for the hour. She had a habit of walking around her car to check for flats before unlocking it and getting in because of a flat tire years ago when she was a medical resident. Everything looked fine. She backed out of her space and drove down the two levels to the exit.

Nothing entered her mind while she drove the half-mile or so to her house, other than doing a mental survey of her closet as she considered what to wear for dinner. Parkview was a casual town but she liked to take the opportunity to wear something more sophisticated than jeans and a sweatshirt.

She was nearing Jay Morrison's home, which was a half-dozen blocks closer to the clinic than her own, when something moving caught her eye. A figure dressed entirely in black moved furtively from the side yard of Jay's house to a dark-colored Camry parked on the street directly in front of the house and jumped in on the passenger side. The car sped off down the street without its lights on, then made a quick left turn onto Louisiana. The driver headed west toward the outskirts of the city, traveling at a high rate of speed. She noted that the house was still draped in police tape because of the ongoing murder investigation; no one should have been skulking around there.

Julia called 911 as she tailed the car, albeit at a slower, safer pace. She wasn't able to read its license plate because it had been obscured by a cover of some kind. She did, however, notice a bright pink reflecting sticker on the left side of the trunk. A flamingo maybe, she thought. Following a half-block behind, she witnessed the driver running through a stop sign before sideswiping a car parked on the street in front of a house at the end of the block ahead. She was hesitant to try to follow any farther because of the Camry's speed. Once the car went another few blocks it would be lost from sight, anyway.

After giving the pertinent details to the 911 dispatcher Julia turned back toward her own home. Her heart palpitated heavily in her chest for a couple of moments. She paused to take some deep, calming breaths before continuing her drive home. Instead of stopping there, however, curious about what might have happened at Jay's house, she circled back and parked her car in the street where the Camry had been waiting. She glanced around to see if anyone was nearby before stepping out of her car. The late fall temperatures in the forties tended to keep everyone inside their warm houses in the evenings. Seeing no one, she slipped into the side yard and approached the window to what she knew from her previous visits to the house was the dining room.

She waited a moment, breathing quietly, and listened for any sounds coming from inside. She leaned her forehead against the window and peeked in. Though it was dark, light spilled in from a lamppost in the neighbor's yard. She could see that all the desk and file drawers had been pulled open. File folders and loose papers littered the floor. *Who had been in here, and what were they looking for?* Julia asked herself. She crept to the back of the house where she tested the back door. It was locked. She looked at the nearby windows and didn't see any evidence of breaking in. It appeared that whoever had been here either had a key or didn't actually enter—which didn't seem likely considering the mess she had witnessed, although it might not have happened just now.

She walked slowly around to the front of the house looking for other windows that might have afforded an entrance into the house but didn't find anything. She returned to the safety of her car and called Nolan for the second time that day. After telling him what she had observed, he said he would call the detective and for Julia to go on home. The detective would contact her later.

Julia drove the several blocks back to her home where Trixie was hopping up and down like a rabbit. After giving her dog some love and ear scratches and filling her bowl with kibbles, Julia got ready for her own dinner with Alex. She pulled on charcoal-gray slacks and a soft, medium-blue sweater while her mind tried to connect the dots surrounding Jay's death. *What was the missing piece that would make everything make sense? What was he, or she, looking for in the house?*

JULIA AND ALEX decided to go to a popular, upscale pub that featured an industrial decor in the adult area upstairs, with a family-friendly theme downstairs. The most recent owners had turned the large space, which had previously housed an Italian restaurant, into a trendy place with great food, a rotating selection of draft beer, and a good, quality house wine.

"You seem like you're far away tonight, Julia," Alex said as they waited for their food to arrive from the downstairs kitchen.

Julia smiled and shrugged. She hadn't yet told him about witnessing someone leaving Jay's house on the short drive over. Several times over the past couple of days she had started to tell him other details she had learned, but had held her tongue. She wasn't sure why--a sixth sense warning perhaps. She took a breath and launched into telling of the evening's incident. There really wasn't much to tell. It was thinking about how it related—or maybe didn't relate—to Jay's untimely death that was the important part.

"Did you know that Jay learned about Parkview from Peter Lewis?" Julia asked between bites of the extra-thin-crust pepperoni pizza, her favorite.

"Yeah, I think Peter told me about that. Is that important?"

Alex finished his beer and ordered a second for each of them when Julia nodded that she too was ready.

"It was a surprise to me, but I suppose he had to have some kind of connection to the town to know to start a business here. Do you know how Peter and Jay knew each other? Did they go to college together?"

"Same college but different graduating classes. Same fraternity though."

"Ah. The *brotherhood* connection." Julia nodded slowly, aware of the tight bonds that often developed between young men in fraternities.

"Are you still helping your nephew with Jay's case? Do they have any new ideas to pursue?"

Julia wiped the last of the pizza sauce off her mouth with the extra napkins brought by the waitress. "Nolan said they're looking into the possibility of unintentional self-induced methanol poisoning, from all the hand sanitizers they found in his house. And there's still the question of the mysterious half-sister and accusations of money missing from the ESCO union pension fund."

Alex scoffed. "Neither of which has yet been proven as fact."

"Nor proven to be false." Julia took a swallow of her beer as her phone came to life with a call from Detective Kilkelly.

"We weren't able to chase down that car you reported but someone could still call in on it. We get a lot of people reporting cars racing up and down the streets. Maybe we'll get lucky and get enough information to locate the Camry."

"That would be nice. Did you check inside Jay's house?"

"Yes. Nolan and I met over there and went inside. Quite a mess. It wasn't like that earlier, at least not the last time I saw it."

"Could you tell if it was broken into?"

"No broken windows, and no reports of security violations, so someone may have had a key."

"As in who?"

"We're checking with his ex-wife. That's all I know right now, Dr. Fairchild."

"Okay. Thanks for calling. Bye."

Alex looked up. "Who was that? It sounded like you were talking to the police."

"Detective Kilkelly was giving me the follow-up on that car I told you about."

Alex scowled. "Don't you worry about getting hurt or something when you get involved in your sleuthing? I worry, even if you don't."

Julia smiled. "That's sweet of you, but I think more of finding out the truth than worrying about anything."

"Well, I don't want to find out that you were murdered because of getting involved."

CHAPTER 15
FOLLOW THE MONEY

Relaxing in her pajamas and robe, Julia started thinking about other ways to fill in the blanks in the investigation. Was it murder? Or was it an accidental death? Thinking about Jay prompted her to call Sophia to see if she had learned any more about Jay's work with Globisphere. It was already after ten o'clock, but Julia figured actresses were accustomed to late nights.

"Oh, Julia. I'm so glad you called. I got the part after all and we start filming my scenes next week."

"That's awesome. I'll be able to say I know a real movie actress," said Julia. "Do you know when this film will be in the movie theaters?"

"That's a big unknown. Sometimes they never get released, but I'm just thrilled to be filming. I'll worry about that other stuff later. For now, I'll focus on studying the script and get ready with my lines."

"I wish you well, Sophia. Somehow I think you'll do a fabulous job."

"Thanks. So what's going on in Parkview?"

"You were going to call Globisphere today. Did you find time to do that?"

"Oh, yes! You're not going to believe what I learned. I hope you're sitting down."

"As a matter of fact, I'm in my jammies sitting in a comfy chair in front of the fireplace. With a glass of wine and a blanket." Julia pulled her feet under her. "What on earth did you find out?"

"You would have been proud of my acting today. I had to do some fast thinking to get this close-mouthed guy to tell me what I wanted to know."

"I'm sure you plied your skills well and charmed this dude. Tell me, already."

"Okay. Jay's job was to recruit stores to sign contracts for these cluster-type malls that Globisphere builds all over the countryside back there. Many of the companies already had stores in other malls so apparently it was pretty easy to sell them on a new location."

"New location, repeat customers. I see that," said Julia.

"Things were going well and the malls' retail spaces were filling up, but after a couple of years some of the companies started complaining that the extras they had paid for weren't being fulfilled."

"What does that mean?"

"It means certain kinds of upgrades, or extra square footage, or preferred location—that kind of thing."

"Okay. Go on."

"This happened enough times that Globisphere's construction manager became alarmed and asked to see the contracts that had been signed by one of their longtime client companies. That's when he discovered that the form turned in by Jay was different from the copy of the form held by the company filing the complaint."

"Uh oh. That sounds like a form of fraud."

"Something like that. Michael, the man I talked to today, said they figured Jay was taking money on the side and making promises he couldn't keep. He had these businesses sign separate contracts for the additional benefits without giving them to Globisphere. How he thought he would get away with it long-term, I don't know."

Julia whistled. "And by the time the construction began several years in the future, Jay would be off somewhere on another project and no one would be the wiser. But he had to know he would get caught sooner or later."

"You don't know Jay like I do. He has—I mean had—a gambler's mind. And no heart when it came to business."

"Maybe no conscience either. In business, I mean."

"I think you're right. What about you? Did you hear from the law firm about the death certificate?"

"Not today. At least I didn't see any faxes come through from them. Since it's an old case, in law-years anyway, the paperwork is probably in one of those boxes like my sister and I sifted through in Seattle. I'll call them on Monday if I don't get a fax by then."

"Sounds like a plan. I hope you'll keep me posted."

"Of course. I just thought of something else. Is your pregnancy going to affect the filming?"

"Not at all. I told the director about it. He said he hopes to be done shooting by the time I show too much. If not, the costume department will figure things out along the way. Otherwise, I'm doing fine. Even if this wasn't in my life plan at this point. I hadn't thought I would be a single mom."

Julia felt tears welling up in her eyes as she thought of one of her high school classmates whose husband, a Washington State Patrol officer, had been murdered when their child was a toddler. Nothing could totally erase the hole in her heart, she'd said. "You'll have a beautiful child who'll be lucky to have you as a mom. Good night, Sophia."

Julia pulled the blanket around her as the fire died down. She ran through her suspect list again, starting with the women. She hadn't been able to fully exclude LeAnne in Jay's death, accidental or not, but she knew in her gut that LeAnne wasn't the right person. Sophia might be an actress but Julia couldn't put her in the hot seat either. Becca had to stay on the list but Julia ranked her as low probability considering her sons would inherit the bulk of the estate anyway.

That still left Greg, who might kill for advancement purposes, and Drake, whose motives could be jealousy or financial loss prevention at his bank. Adam Johns from the union certainly had motive, at least in Julia's opinion. He wanted someone to be accountable for the financial losses in the pension account. And he was a hothead, by report.

Julia didn't feel strongly in favor of any of the three for being the "trigger," but who else was there? If for no other reason than Sophia and her baby, Julia felt honor-bound to figure out the rest of the story around Jay's demise. But how was she going to do that? It was like waiting for the answer to fall out of the sky. In the gloom of a Pacific Northwest October day, rain was much more likely.

THE STORMY WEATHER was enough to keep Julia from taking her usual morning run. She could always run later in the day if the rain let up, she reasoned. The bank statements that hadn't jibed with each other nagged at her conscience. She finally called one of her fellow dancers who worked in account management at the River City bank. The main branch on Broadway had open hours on Saturdays. Angela Rogers was happy to meet with her to review the statements for ESCO's account as long as someone with proper authority gave permission. Julia called Nolan, who said he could meet her at the bank in an hour with the paperwork to allow them access to the account.

In the past, Julia had occasionally experienced a strange, fluttery sensation in her chest that seemed to occur shortly before unexpected happy or exciting news. This was one of those moments. She didn't know what had triggered the mysterious sense of premonition, but it was the same sign that had presented itself prior to those other events. She danced around the kitchen in her excitement. It felt like her heart was racing but a quick pulse check told her it was beating at its normal rate of sixty. She wished she had someone to tell. Trixie opened an eye but otherwise ignored her mistress.

ONCE SHE HAD VERIFIED the authorization, Angela did something magical on the computer and opened the account that matched the statements that Julia had found at Jay's house. Julia was always impressed by technical skills beyond hers. No one would accuse her of being a computer nerd. Drake had given Julia a copy of the final statement from Parkview National Bank, which she now shared with Angela.

Angela spent several long minutes at the computer, frowning at times and smiling now and then. With a big "Aha" and a giant grin, she turned the screen around for Julia and Nolan to see what she was excited about. "Here's what I think happened inside this account. First, I verified that the final balance of the account at Parkview National was equal to the opening balance here. It had been an electronic transfer, and all went like it was supposed to." She pointed out the number on the screen and Drake's printed statement.

"Something unusual happened between the opening of the

account and the next statement date. A hundred and fifty thousand dollars was transferred to another checking account."

Julia felt her heart rate jump. She noticed Nolan leaning forward more in his chair. Julia asked, "How do you know? Can you tell where it went?"

She smiled grimly. "Yes and no. The acronym ACH on this line is the transaction code for money transferred to a checking account. I don't have a way of knowing which account, however. I'll have to refer this to the investigation team, which only works Monday through Friday. All I can tell you now is that it isn't in any account at *this* bank."

Julia looked at the statements from Jay's house. "I have a feeling you'll find another withdrawal like that later. Drake said about four hundred and twenty-five thousand dollars was missing, according to his calculations."

"You're right, Julia. Another three hundred thousand dollars was transferred out seven months later, which was August of last year."

Julia and Nolan looked at each other. "It looks like we have some more work to do," said Nolan. "None of us has had the time to pursue this line of thinking with the short-staffing of both the police and sheriff departments and the recent heavy load of cases."

"Maybe Sandy Lantz's comments about offshore accounts meant something after all," said Julia.

"How long will it take to get the information on those money transfers?" Nolan asked Angela.

Angela leaned back in her office chair. "It can take up to ninety days under normal circumstances but I'll put a rush on it. It's still going to take some time."

"Thank you. I'll get back to you next week if that's all right," said Nolan.

"Thanks, Angela," said Julia. "I'll see you at dance class soon."

Nolan walked his aunt to her car. "It might be that Jay's death comes down to money, after all."

"There's the old adage that says something about 'following the money,'" said Julia. "There's the money Jay inherited from his father, half of which should have gone to LeAnne, and now almost a half-million dollars of ESCO pension money unaccounted for. And Jay's hands are in both of those pockets."

"You're right. I'll talk with Greg Lantz on Monday. And, yes, I'll let you know what I find out. And, no, I don't know anything more about the prowler at Jay's house. Is there anything else you want to know?"

Julia grinned. "How's the baby?"

CHAPTER 16

MACGROGGERY GROG

J ulia saw her neighbor waving at her as she pulled into her driveway. She noticed Ellie had made major headway in her effort to reclaim the landscaping in her front yard. Julia crossed the narrow residential street between their homes to compliment her on the improvement.

"Your yard is looking like you've had a professional work on it," said Julia.

Ellie laughed. "That would be thanks to your teaching. It takes a lot of physical effort, but I enjoy chilling out here in nature. I'm grateful for a few days of dry weather so I can get it done. Then I'll leave it till next spring."

"Anyway, good job. How are things going for you? We haven't had a chance to talk since that day a couple of weeks ago."

"Can't complain, but I wanted to tell you about the other night when someone shot at your house. When the police came by and asked if I had seen or heard anything I told them about hearing the motorcycle. I was in the kitchen and didn't see anything from there. But I remembered later that I saw someone lurking in your yard near the side entrance."

"When was that?" Julia felt her heart speed up as goose pimples popped up on her arms, even though she was wearing a warm jacket.

"I'm sure it was a couple of evenings before the shooting. I didn't see a strange car parked in front of your house and I wondered if he, or maybe it was she, had ridden a bicycle instead."

"Can you describe this person?"

Ellie laughed nervously. "I'm going to sound like the typical witness. He, or she, was about five-foot eight, medium build, dressed all in black with a hooded sweatshirt. I didn't see a logo on the shirt."

Julia grinned. "You're right. The *usual* description. Did you call the police?"

"I was going to but by the time I went inside and got my cell phone they were already gone. I didn't really have much to tell, anyway."

"So you didn't see them leave."

"No. Or hear them. I think that's why I thought they might have been on a bike. Or their car was parked down the street. The street parking spaces are always full because so many of these historic houses have a one-car garage and the owners have two cars, so I wouldn't have noticed a strange car."

"That could have been the same night someone shot at Drake's house," said Julia. "I wonder if it was the same person."

"Is it bad that I didn't call the police that night, Julia?"

Julia sighed. "It might have been helpful then, but it's too late to do anything now except report it to the detective, which I can do myself. They might not have found anything even if they had come that evening. Is it okay if they come over to talk with you if they decide to check it out?"

"Of course. I'm sorry I didn't tell you right away."

"Well, thank you for the information. Talk to you soon."

Julia walked through the lawn toward her side entrance which opened into the sunroom. She surveyed the shrubs looking for something obvious like a piece of fabric torn from a jacket but didn't see anything reportable. She decided to tell Nolan about it anyway. Perhaps it would be useful information later when added to the other bits he and Detective Kilkelly had already collected.

"Thanks for the information, Aunt Julia. I'll pass that on to Kilkelly."

"Do you think you'll talk with my neighbor?"

"Probably not right now, unless you think she has additional details to share. Or if it would make you feel better."

"I'm sure she told me everything she knows."

"Okay. Hey, did you hear the report on the hand sanitizer analysis? I thought the detective might talk to you about it."

"Not yet. What did you learn?" Julia barely breathed. "Were they heavily tainted?"

"I kinda hoped that's what the lab report would say, but they found only traces of methanol in one of them."

"Not enough to cause Jay's methanol poisoning, then." Julia let out a long sigh. "Back to finding another source, I'm afraid. Did you ever find out who Jay's Friday night visitor was? I remember you said that one of his golfing partners mentioned it and that they drank grog together."

"I'm afraid not. We interviewed the neighbors but nobody had noticed anything unusual. So many cars park in the street it's hard to tell which house they might belong to. Or if they're just visiting. Or *whom* they're visiting."

"And if that person was the source of the methanol, as in

poisoned grog, he or she isn't going to be coming forward anytime soon."

"Right. I think we're going to have to catch a lucky break to find out who that was."

"As I see it, bad guys usually reveal themselves sooner or later," said Julia.

"Yeah. I hope it's sooner. I want to get back on regular patrol and be done with this investigative work."

"Same here. Good luck, Nolan. I'll let you know if I have any new clues for you."

Julia made herself a cup of peppermint tea and sat in her big chair. She considered making a fire but felt the urge to pursue the idea of the grog having been tainted. She had heard about the distillery across the Columbia River and that there had been some prominent local investors. Their website indicated they were open on Saturdays until five p.m. Julia called Carly who was game to check it out with her.

JULIA AND CARLY arrived at the MacGroggery Distillery in time to catch the end of a tour that was in the tasting room. They listened as the guide, Bryce MacGregor according to the name tag, appropriately attired in a working man's kilt and a plaid tam, described the distinctive taste of each of their products. The enthusiastic people in his audience nodded and smiled as they sipped the samples offered by a young hostess. Julia felt her tongue wrinkle as she tasted one of the strong whiskeys. She noticed Carly making a face.

At the last tasting station, he launched into the story of how he and his partner came up with their newest concoction, the MacGrog. His face glowed with pride as he narrated the history of the brew, ostensibly recreated from an old family recipe that had been passed down from one MacGregor to another. Once again, the pretty hostess sporting a plaid apron (MacGregor tartan?) dispensed small plastic cups of the golden-brown liquid to the members of the group.

Julia hesitated before taking a sip. She couldn't help but wonder if the grog that Jay had supposedly drunk was the true source of the methanol. Putting her worry aside, she took a swallow. The amber liquid was smoother than she expected and had a pleasant taste which surprised her. She caught Carly smiling as she tasted her own portion.

Their host reminded the guests they could purchase the beverages if they chose, and to drive safely. Julia caught his attention as he began to walk toward another door labeled Employees Only.

"Hi, ma'am. Bryce MacGregor here. How can I help you?" He took off his Scottish tam and smiled broadly. Julia swore that with his curly red hair and blue eyes he could have arrived from Scotland last week, though his language skills were pure American.

Julia and Carly had discussed how she should broach her concern and decided that telling the truth would work best, so that's what she did. She concluded her narrative with a question about local investors, hoping to learn with whom Jay may have shared a drink.

"There are quite a few of them around. Some guys, like a group of golfers from the Parkview Country Club, pooled their money and invested a few thousand dollars. One of the banks —well, not the bank, but a guy who worked at the bank— dumped one hundred thousand dollars into the kitty."

"Would that have been Jay Morrison?" Julia felt her palms get sweaty.

"No, not that bank. It was Drake Ashford from Parkview National. Why?"

. . .

JULIA BOUGHT A PINT of the grog so Nolan and Kilkelly would know what to look for when they searched Drake's house. She had to ease her foot off the gas several times as she and Carly drove the thirty miles from St. Helens back to Parkview. Her heart raced as she tried to put all the missing pieces into place.

"Carly, where would Drake get one hundred thousand dollars to invest? Do you think he makes that much money to have saved up that kind of cash?"

"That sounds more like what his annual salary might be, but I suppose he gets bonuses for performance."

"And he's divorced so he's probably paying child support, which would eat up some of his salary. And maybe college tuitions if his kids are old enough. I could ask Pam. She might know."

"That sounds like a good idea," said Carly. "Could it be union pension money? Adam Johns was worried about that loss of funds. Could that be where the money came from?"

"Probably not. Nolan and I went over the statements with Angie at the bank. She was able to confirm that the initial transfers were done correctly, and that the money losses occurred *after* the accounts were at Jay's bank. So it doesn't look like Drake profited illegally at that point."

"Maybe Drake was threatening to disclose something he knew about Jay," said Carly.

"Like blackmail? If that's true, I wonder what he knew and how he found out about it."

"Could he have learned about Jay's spurious side contracts at Globisphere and those offshore accounts?"

"And threatened to tell somebody if Jay didn't pay him, say one hundred thousand dollars?"

"Money's a powerful motivator, I hear." Carly clicked her tongue.

Julia looked at Carly. "We need to find out where the one hundred thousand dollars came from."

"If Drake is guilty of anything, won't your friend Pam be unhappy with you? I assume they're still dating, since you haven't said otherwise."

"Probably for a while, but I can't look the other way if he's guilty of something."

"I know. Hopefully she'll understand. Eventually."

CHAPTER 17

DEAD OR ALIVE?

J ulia reported to Nolan what she and Carly had learned at the distillery. She had expected him to go to Drake's house immediately and search for a bottle of the grog. She had even emailed a picture of the distinctive bottle to help him. Instead, they discussed due diligence, after which Nolan told her that he and Detective Kilkelly would do their own investigation into the distillery, which would involve working with the proper authorities across the river. Then, if they believed it prudent, they would talk with Drake.

Julia had to admit that she couldn't come up with a plausible explanation for Drake to have been involved in Jay's death. She had wondered earlier if there had been improprieties in how Drake had managed the ESCO pension money that Jay had uncovered. The visit with the account manager at the bank that morning seemed to suggest that Jay, not Drake, may have been up to something. If that were the case, it was more likely that Jay, not Drake, had something to hide. In which case there was no reason for Drake to kill Jay—he could just expose him.

Julia felt a headache coming on. Had Jay been hiding something? Was it the money from his stint at Globisphere? Was it the inheritance he failed to share with his sister, who appeared to be very much alive despite the death certificate? Was it the $425,000 missing from the ESCO account? And, the biggest question, did someone else know? And who? Was there another person involved who didn't want the world to know of their nefarious scheme? And did they cause his death? Was Greg Lantz at the bottom of it, considering his second-hand comment about offshore accounts?

A fresh cup of cappuccino worked on the headache. Julia felt refreshed enough by five o'clock to call LeAnne and see if she was free for dinner, hoping she hadn't traveled to see her mother over the weekend.

The early dinner crowd was light for a Saturday. Julia and LeAnne scored a booth, much to Julia's delight. Grant's Restaurant had live music for happy hour. A young man with long hair in a ponytail played classical music on an acoustic guitar. The volume was moderate, just enough to create a pleasant ambiance without interfering with conversation. Learning how to play a guitar was on Julia's bucket list. Surely it was easier than playing piano, which she had done since third grade.

"It feels like a week since we talked but it's only been two days," said Julia. "Right? Wasn't it Thursday morning?"

"Yes. I was hoping you were calling because you finally figured out what was going on. Or at least proved that I was alive." LeAnne laughed and raised her glass to Julia's.

"The detective is looking into the death certificate. He'll find out who filed it, I think, and when."

"I've already submitted a DNA swab that will be compared to whatever they have on Jay. That should prove something."

The waiter arrived with their dinners. Julia had ordered the salmon, which was always grilled to perfection in her experience. LeAnne was fond of shrimp and requested the scampi. "Thank you," said Julia when the waiter offered fresh ground pepper for their salads. For the next few minutes they enjoyed the succulent food and wine, reveling in what felt like special treatment at the popular restaurant. Julia had been an early aficionado of the restaurant and knew several of the waitstaff and the owner by name.

"Do you have any new information, like where the methanol came from?"

"Not yet. It wasn't in the hand sanitizer after all." Julia shared what she and Carly had learned at the distillery and what the detective and Nolan were planning to do.

"I'm curious about what you might know about the money that was deposited in your mom's bank account all those years. Like how often, or how much, or from which bank? Do you have any information at all?"

"Mom's memory isn't as good as it used to be and she said she didn't care about the details because she knew it was from my father and that's all she needed to know. I do know it was always the same amount, three thousand dollars, and always on the first day of the month. It came through as a transfer from another bank, but she didn't know which one because the name wasn't listed. It was all in bank code, I'm sure. She assumed it was meant to help her raise me. When the money kept coming long after I was out of college, she wondered why, but just kept it in a separate account. She said she always planned to give it to me instead of spending it on herself."

"Did she ever get married?" Julia signaled to the waiter for two more glasses of cabernet.

"She did, but it didn't last. He traveled with his job and forgot to come home sometimes." LeAnne looked off into the distance with a wistful smile. "She never stopped loving Will, I think, even though I don't think they ever talked again after I was born. Or if they did, she didn't tell me."

Julia smiled. "That's a true love story."

"He must have been pretty awesome to support my mom and me all those years. I wish I had known him."

"It makes me wonder how he had such a skanky son."

"Maybe those genes were from the mom, whoever she was."

Julia and LeAnne giggled a moment, then Julia asked, "Do you suppose your mom still has any old bank statements that show those deposits? If she does, Angela—who works at Jay's bank—might be able to trace them and find out where they originated."

"For what reason?" LeAnne looked puzzled.

"I'm curious about when the payments stopped. If they were automatic payments out of an account, I'd like to know who stopped them."

"I'll ask her. I wouldn't be surprised to find out she has them. She saves everything."

JULIA PACED in the kitchen while her coffee brewed. She wanted to get her hands on LeAnne's mom's bank statements but couldn't do anything with them until Monday, when Angela would be at the bank. She considered going to her office to check for a fax from the law firm in Hartford but doubted anyone was working overtime to respond to her request.

Finally, after two mugs of high-test coffee, she pulled on her gardening outerwear and grabbed her pruners. She decided to tackle the vine maple that had started to grow into the neighbor's *arborvitae*. She studied the overall shape of the tree, marveling at its tenacity in sprouting new branches wherever she had lopped off an offending limb. She debated whether she should just chop it down, which would be difficult without a chainsaw, or prune it severely now and borrow a chainsaw to cut it down in the spring.

She struggled with the thicker limbs and resolved to get back to the gym to work with a trainer on upper body strength. Or she could wait and use a chainsaw. Once she had created breathing space between the maple and the *arborvitae*, she called it quits.

"Looking good," Ellie said from her front yard. "Isn't it nice to have another dry day to do final yard cleanup for the winter?"

"Yes, and to have it coincide with a day off." They both laughed.

"Any luck with finding that motorcycle?"

"Not yet. It would be total luck for the police to find it. And I'm not expecting miracles."

"I hope they find the guy who's been creeping around houses. I've been keeping my doors locked even when I'm home."

"Nowadays that's a good idea. My hands are getting cold so I'm calling it a day and going in. Talk to you later."

JULIA SAT down in her den with the probated will and its attachments. She read each page, carefully looking for any bit that didn't jibe. The death certificate looked legitimate despite its presumably having been forged somehow. She knew professional forgers could create any document requested, for a price, but perhaps someone had made a mistake on this one. She wished she had a proper legal document for comparison.

Then Julia remembered that she had a copy of her dad's death certificate. "Where did I put it?" she asked herself aloud. Trixie jerked her head up at the sound of Julia's voice. She found the file folder in which she kept personal documents and searched for the envelope that contained a copy of her father's will, his death certificate, a list of the beneficiaries, and an accounting of his assets.

She placed the two death certificates side by side and inspected them closely. She squealed when she noticed that the fonts were different despite theoretically being from the same agency. The notation in the lower right corner designating the form number was missing as well on the forged certificate.

Nolan picked up on the first ring.

"I can prove that LeAnne's death certificate is a phony," she said.

"How did you manage that?"

"If you're free to come by I'll show you. Detective Kilkelly might want to see this too."

"Okay. One or both of us will be there in about thirty minutes. Hope you're right, Aunt Julia."

Julia jotted down a few other details to check while she waited. The doctor's signature would have been forged as well. That would be easy to check because each physician has a unique identifier that follows his or her name, necessary because so many professionals have stylized signatures which were often impossible to read. Julia made a copy of her father's death certificate and circled the items she thought would help Nolan and Kilkelly in their due diligence.

With the copies of both death certificates in front of her guests, Julia explained what she had noticed when she examined the forms closely.

"This certainly looks like a forgery, but it still doesn't tell us who killed Jay," said Nolan addressing Kilkelly.

"No, but it should help LeAnne claim her share of inheritance from Jay's estate when it goes to probate," said Julia.

"And that's good," said Nolan.

"When I get the rest of the legal papers from the law firm that filed the death certificate," said Julia, "I'm sure LeAnne will have more than enough ammunition to support her claim."

"In case you're wondering, we're following up on the grog that came from MacGroggery's," said Nolan. "Then we can talk to Drake."

"Okay. I hope you'll let me know what you find out. You might as well ask for a complete list of investors. Might save time later."

CHAPTER 18
ADDRESSEE UNKNOWN

The margarita tasted delicious and the chicken burrito was excellent but Julia couldn't shake her glum mood to enjoy her Sunday dinner with Alex.

"What's wrong? You've hardly talked tonight and that's not like you."

Julia sighed. "I'm frustrated with trying to figure out who wanted Jay dead. I'm sure someone was responsible for poisoning him with methanol and I'm puzzled as to who it was and how they did it."

"It's still not your problem, you know."

"I know but I don't like loose ends. I must be missing some essential piece of information."

"Tell me what you know so far. Maybe I can help."

Julia brightened and gave him a rundown of the latest bits of information.

"Are you sure about the amount of money missing from the ESCO account? That's a big chunk of change."

"Drake said that the bank statements were prepared in such a way that it wasn't obvious that the money was missing.

It was itemized in a certain way so that the value of the account looked intact."

"And you said the transfers were done several months apart so it might not be obvious, especially with clever accounting."

"Right. Angela was going to do more tracking tomorrow to try to locate where it went. I hope to hear from her soon after that."

"Any more on that half-sister situation? Did she contact that attorney in Seattle who I recommended?"

Julia smiled. "She shouldn't have any trouble trying to prove her existence after the phony death certificate surfaced."

"What do you mean?" His face flattened.

"Nolan is checking the death certificate against the Washington State records. I haven't heard what he found out yet. But I did prove the certificate presented in the probate was a phony."

"You and Nolan have been busy." Alex took a long swallow of his drink.

"Playing detective is second nature to a physician. We do it every day in our practice of figuring out what's wrong with our patients."

THOUGH PREPARED TO BE DISAPPOINTED WHEN she checked the stack of mail on her desk Monday morning, she was elated to find a cover letter from Dox & Codge, LLC. She had to search through several pages of legal disclaimers to find the rest of the fax and was beginning to think there wasn't an attachment after all. She let out a sigh of relief when she spotted the ten or so extra pages. She read them twice through carefully, hoping to find something that would answer some of her questions.

In addition to a copy of the death certificate which she

had seen before, there was a letter documenting attempts to contact *said heir* Melissa LeAnne Carlton, as her cousin, Drew, had mentioned a few days earlier. It was accompanied by photocopies of two envelopes stamped with *addressee unknown*. Both addresses were in Seattle. Julia guessed that one of them was the last known address of Gloria Carlton. She would ask LeAnne. The letter outlined the process that had been taken to satisfy the legal requirement that all reasonable attempts be made to contact Melissa LeAnne Carlton before assigning the entire estate to William J. Morrison, Jr.

Julia paused when she read the list of names of the attorneys in the sidebar. A Peter Lewis was in the middle of the twenty or so names. If this was the same Peter, he had been a member of the law firm in Hartford at the time. She wondered when he had moved to Parkview, and why? And how much further back did his professional relationship with Jay go? She called Nolan, who asked her to fax the material to him.

Julia whizzed through her morning patients, eager to have a chance to call Becca Morrison. She, of all people, would know the background of Jay and Peter's relationship. And Julia hoped that she still had Becca as an ally in the pursuit of identifying Jay's killer.

"Hey. I just saw a letter that puts Peter Lewis in Hartford the same time that Jay lived there. That was news to me. Do you know the history on that?"

"Sure. I think I told you they were fraternity brothers and all that. Peter is from that area and joined a law firm straight out of school. Jay decided to start his working career in Hartford and Peter's father, who was an exec at Globisphere, helped Jay get a job with them."

"That makes sense."

"What kind of letter are you talking about, anyway?"

"It was something that the detective had. I don't remember any other details."

"Why would he have had a letter about Peter?"

"It wasn't about Peter. It was connected to Jay." Julia crossed her fingers behind her back.

"Hm. Was it a letter of recommendation for a job? Peter might have written something when Jay was applying for his job."

"It was probably something like that. I forgot how long ago that would have been. Do you know?"

"I'm not sure, but he started there not long after he graduated from Yale with his MBA. That was in 2005, I think. Before I knew him."

"Are you from that area too?"

"No, I'm from Philadelphia. I was working for an investment company in Hartford when I met Jay."

"That's right. Sophia said something about you having a background in accounting and planning to get your CPA."

Becca scoffed. "Funny thing. I didn't realize at the time I would be supporting myself again in the future or I would have taken the tests right out of school."

"Good luck to you on those. I've heard they're pretty tough."

"I'll brush up for sure. My employer said I would have some study time and the company will pay for the tests, so I feel fortunate. Gotta run. Let me know if you need anything else."

Julia squeezed in one more call during her lunch break. She wanted to confirm LeAnne's mom's addresses in Seattle and ask her about the old bank accounts.

"I don't recognize either of those addresses at all. It's not even close to where we lived. She only moved once and that was long after I was out of high school."

"I didn't think to Google them at the time, but I'll do that in a bit and see if they're even legitimate addresses."

"Good idea."

"What about those bank statements?"

"Mom said she found a couple of them and took them to FedEx. I tried to talk her through taking a picture with her camera and sending them by email but she couldn't figure it out. Sorry for that! I know you wanted them right away."

"No problem. Mail from Seattle should only take a couple of days. I'll ask Angela at the bank to look at the statements when you get them to me."

"What exactly are you hoping to find out?"

"I'm following a trail that I hope will help me to prove that Jay knew of your existence and purposefully eliminated you as an heir by deceit."

"Because?"

"It's the principle of the idea. If there's proof that Jay took steps to deny you your share of your father's estate, I want to find it. You can use it when Jay's will goes to probate. Then you'll want to do a consultation with one of the attorneys on that list from my cousin and find out what will be required to file. This will help your case and save some work on an attorney's part. And save you the money that they would have had to spend on the research."

"I wonder if there's any money left from my father's estate. It sounds like Jay spent millions getting his bank started."

"That's something an attorney can help with."

"I hate to take anything away from Becca and her boys. What if this hurts them?"

"You have a kind heart, LeAnne. But remember that Becca already got her divorce settlement and should be okay financially. This is about correcting a wrongful deed. Maybe you won't get any money, but I have a feeling you will. Once Angela can trace those accounts we'll know more."

LeAnne sighed. "I know you're right. I'll get the statements to you after they arrive."

JULIA CALLED Nolan as soon as she was done with her clinic for the day and told him about the documents from the Hartford law firm.

"Are you sure it's the Peter Lewis that we know?"

"Yes, I am. I called Becca and asked if Peter and Jay had both worked in Hartford and she confirmed that they had. They were frat brothers; I think you knew that already. She told me that Peter's father helped Jay get his first job. It makes me wonder if there's been any other collusion between them since that episode."

Nolan tsked. "You have a suspicious mind."

"It's a logical question if you think about it. If Peter knew that Jay had concealed knowledge of his half-sister then, I would think he might have had his hands in other ventures of Jay's."

"Having his name listed on the firm's office stationery doesn't prove that Peter was involved if it's not his signature. Or that he was aware of this incident. That would require investigating something that happened at least four years ago. I'm sure Kilkelly isn't going to authorize anything like that."

"I understand. But it's clear, to me at least, that someone in Peter's office was involved when Jay's father died."

CHAPTER 19

CONNECTING THE DOTS

J ulia's eyes scanned the traffic around her as she drove across town to make rounds to see her nursing home patients, which she did every eight weeks as required by law. She realized that, for the last several days, she had been unconsciously looking for a dark Camry with a pink decal on the left rear quarter panel whenever she was in her car. She laughed at herself as she pulled into the parking lot of The Royal Manor. *Fat chance I'll ever see it. Maybe I could ask St. Anthony for help,* she thought to herself.

The evening staff greeted her cordially and handed her the charts for her patients, Julia having called ahead to let them know she was coming. Two of them were housed on the rehabilitation wing where residents recovered from surgery for fractured hips or shoulder replacement. Those patients were typically elderly and often lived alone. In addition to the physical therapy, they needed extra assistance until they could manage the so-called activities of daily living.

Julia had several other longer-term residents who likely

would live out their lives in the facility. Some of them had families nearby but the care they required was more demanding than an equally old spouse could manage. Some were totally alone. Other than the nursing staff, for those few patients Julia was often their only company. She enjoyed visiting with them while she evaluated them relative to their medical issues.

Back in the car, she said a quick prayer of thanks for her own excellent health and asked for special blessings for Doris, Simon, Gladys, Tony, and Edward, all of whom she'd visited that evening. She knew that some of her colleagues felt that nursing home rounds were boring and depressing but she always felt uplifted. She did her best to fuss over her patients and let them know she cared about them. Nothing depressing about that.

Julia's mind wandered to thinking about Jay and Becca and LeAnne and Sophia as she crossed town toward home. She was lost in thought while sitting at a red light on Washington Way but perked up when she saw a flash of pink on the back end of a charcoal-gray Camry as it crossed from right to left in front of the car ahead of her. She recognized the pink ribbon of a breast cancer decal. She waited for the light to turn green, then moved into the left turn lane to follow the sedan. She traveled a couple of blocks without spotting it, then had to wait for another red light. She drummed her fingers on the steering wheel as she used her mental powers to make the light change to green more quickly.

She was finally freed from the traffic signal's power and scooted down the street. She didn't see anything resembling the car for the several blocks ahead of her. *Maybe the driver is eating out tonight,* Julia surmised. She turned left onto Commerce Avenue where several popular restaurants were located. Nothing. *Damn!* Julia rarely swore out loud but now and again she let herself *think* an appropriate word.

For the next several minutes she drove up and down the main streets of the downtown core but didn't see any other charcoal Camrys, let alone the one she wanted. She called Nolan from her car and told him what she'd seen. He promised to relay the information to the detective so more eyes would be on the lookout.

JULIA GAVE Trixie some dog-love and fed her before she checked the mail. She rarely got real mail anymore, mostly mailers and the occasional statement that she didn't get online. One large mailing envelope from FedEx stood out because it had a hand-written address and a personalized label from Gloria Carlton in the upper left corner. It was stamped *priority overnight delivery*. Julia smiled as she ripped it open. LeAnne's mother had been resourceful and found another way to send the documents expeditiously without having to use email. Ms. Carlton had enclosed three separate statements. She had taken the time to circle the deposits that had come from Will Morrison. As LeAnne had told her, they were the same amount every time and always on the first day of the month.

Julia wished she could go to the bank and have Angela do her tracing magic. Instead, she called Pam to catch up and tell her about spotting the Camry.

"Are you sure it's the same one you saw at Jay's house?"

"No, but it had a pink decal on the bumper and was dark charcoal. It was a breast cancer sticker which makes more sense than a flamingo I'd thought it might be, I suppose."

"Don't you have a pink plastic flamingo in your backyard? I'm sure I saw one by your goldfish pond."

"Yeah, but that's not the same as a flamingo on a car. We don't live in Florida, you know."

Pam laughed. "A breast cancer decal would make sense. I see them everywhere. But if it was a guy sneaking around the yard, why would he be jumping into a car with a breast cancer sign? That seems more like a woman's thing."

"Maybe it was a girlfriend's or even a wife's car. Or it could have been a woman in black doing the sneaking around and driving. I couldn't tell if it was a male or female."

"Hopefully someone will spot it. Did you see any license plate numbers?"

"I was at the wrong angle to see them because I was behind another car. It would have helped to have seen even a partial plate. Oh, well. So what's up with Drake? Is he back to normal yet?"

"Seems to be more like himself. We went out to dinner Saturday and had a good time. He and I both like Grant's. And he didn't cringe when we ran into Greg and Sandy Lantz, who were leaving as we arrived."

"That sounds like progress."

"Yeah. They talked a little banking business and that was it."

"Anything new on his shooting incident?"

"Same as on yours. Not enough to go on."

Julia told her about the bank statements that she planned to take to the bank the next day for Angela to investigate. With a promise to get together the following weekend, Julia ended the call and poured herself a glass of wine. It was too late to go to her Monday evening dance class, anyway. She made a mental list of the loose ends of her case and settled into reading a book she'd picked up by Louise Penny, one of her favorite mystery novelists. She wished her own mystery would be solved soon.

. . .

THE NEXT MORNING on her way to work Julia left the bank statements with the concierge at River City Bank with a note for Angela to call her as soon as she knew something. She drove on to her clinic with an optimistic feeling that Ms. Carlton's documents would be helpful. She hoped that the person who had closed the old account or stopped the automatic payments would be identified in short order. The accounts where the union's missing money went—likely to offshore accounts, she figured—were also on her mind. She hoped Angela had been able to trace those as well.

Nolan poked his head into her office mid-morning with an update on the death certificate. "You were right about it being a forgery. The birthdate was a couple of days off and the doctor's identification number doesn't exist in the system."

Julia retrieved the file containing the recent documents and handed Nolan the letter that accompanied the death certificate that she'd mentioned to him earlier. "What do you think about this?" She pointed to Peter Lewis' name on the sidebar.

Nolan whistled. "I'll have a talk with him."

"Maybe Peter is our mystery grog drinker."

"Or maybe it's a coincidence that he happened to work as a lawyer in that company."

Julia jumped when she heard a loud rap on the door.

"Excuse me, Dr. Fairchild, but Angela from the bank asked me to interrupt you," said Amie. "She's on line one."

"Hi, Angela. I'm putting you on speaker so Nolan, the deputy sheriff, can hear you," said Julia.

"You're not going to believe what I discovered," said Angela. "I was so surprised I double-checked to be sure."

"We're all ears," said Julia, glancing at Nolan.

"You remember that there were several six-figure transfers

out of the ESCO account according to our River City statements."

"Yes, and…"

"The account into which they were transferred belongs to Jay Morrison. A personal account."

"Somehow that doesn't surprise me," said Julia.

"What if I told you that there's more than twenty million dollars in the account?"

"*That* surprises me. That's a big number." Julia looked at Nolan, who mimed a whistle and widened his eyes. "Can you tell where the money came from, other than ESCO, of course?"

"No, but I can tell you that the account was opened about ten years ago at another bank and then transferred here when River City Bank opened. It has had multiple other deposits over the years. Some very big ones, according to the agent from the original bank with whom I spoke."

Julia looked at Nolan as she said. "That's about the time Jay was working for Globisphere in Hartford, before he moved to Parkview."

"I've requested additional information through proper channels. That's all I can tell you for now about that account."

"What about the bank statements from Ms. Carlton? Did you get a chance to look at those? I left them with the concierge because you weren't there yet."

"So *that's* what those statements were all about. I haven't done anything with them yet. I'll tackle that project after lunch and a staff meeting. I promise."

"Thanks, Angela," said Julia. "Let me know when you know more."

Julia sat back in her chair and crossed her arms. "I wonder if Becca knows about that account. And if it's the same one Greg Lantz was referring to. It isn't an offshore account, but still…have you talked to him yet?"

"No, but I'll make it a priority and get it done quickly. I didn't think the comment about offshore accounts would be such a big deal but twenty million dollars is a lot of moolah. Who'd have thought there would be this kind of money attached to anyone here in Parkview?"

"And at River City Bank."

CHAPTER 20
ANOTHER BUNNY TRAIL

J ulia wrestled with the idea of calling Alex. She wanted to know if he was aware of Peter's history with Jay in Hartford. She hadn't talked with him since their Sunday Mexican dinner. They had typically talked in the evenings a couple of times during the week for a few minutes before the whole thing involving Jay had erupted. Alex had seemed more distant than usual but she chalked it up to her own preoccupation with solving the unknowns. She tossed a penny in the air and called tails. And dialed Alex's number.

He answered, "Hey. It's been a rough couple of weeks, with Jay dying and all. I'm glad you called. I wasn't sure how you felt about the whole mess."

Julia's heart softened. She hadn't realized how much she missed talking to him. "It *is* a mess for sure. At this point, I'm not sure I want to know if someone was truly responsible for his demise, as opposed to it being an accident of life. I want it to just go away and let life go back to normal."

"Same here. Peter has been inundated with handling the details of Jay's will, the estate, the challenges from Sophia and

LeAnne, and trying to help Becca. I'm helping him as the executor but my part is easy. Most wills are simple compared to what's happening with this one."

"I hear ya. Kilkelly from the Parkview Police department and Nolan—you know, my nephew from the County Sheriff's office? Anyway, they've both been tracking clues from every which direction. Nolan told me he'd much rather be doing his normal job of driving up and down the roads of his territory and writing the occasional ticket. This is more grueling than his usual work. And he's doing it in addition to his usual duty."

"That would be tough. Any closer to figuring out who wanted Jay dead?"

"That list is about the same. But wanting someone dead and doing something to make it happen are two different things."

Alex chuckled. "And that's what keeps attorneys in business."

"I thought it was keeping the sheriff's department and police busy."

"That too."

"Agreed. Part of the reason I called is to ask you about Peter's work when he lived in Hartford. Do you know anything about that?"

"Do you mean specifics? Or in general?"

"Either." Julia wasn't ready to tell him about the letter and death certificate in case they were to become an issue in the probate hearings down the road, considering that Alex was officially involved as executor of the estate. She didn't want to muddy the water.

Alex related the same story that Becca had shared earlier.

"Didn't you tell me that you worked in Hartford as well before you came here? Did you work with Peter?"

"Yes, but not in his law firm. I was employed by Globisphere as an in-house attorney. We occasionally outsourced work to Dox and Codge when we needed their expertise."

Julia felt her antennae twitch. She sat up straighter in her chair. "Did you know Jay when he worked there?"

"How did you know that he worked for Globisphere?"

"Um. Becca mentioned it once when I asked her where they had lived prior to moving here."

"Oh, okay. I didn't know him well. He was part of the contracts team and spent most of his time on the road trying to fill up the retail spaces in the malls that were going to be built."

"I suppose it was a huge company."

"A couple thousand employees, I think. I'm not sure I even met Jay back then. Except at a Christmas party maybe, with five hundred other people." He laughed.

"Sounds pretty impersonal."

"The corporate offices were spread out all over the city. I had little contact with anyone other than the suits when they needed legal guidance or wanted a contract written up."

Julia's cell alerted that Carly was calling. "Hey—my sister is calling. Thanks for the chat. See you Friday?"

"Sure."

"What's up, sis?"

"There's some talk at the ESCO mill about the union filing a formal complaint against the River City Bank. Adam Johns, the guy who's done most of the interacting with the bank, told my husband, Rob, that he's not getting any satisfaction from the vice president, Greg Lantz. They think a lawsuit is the only way to force action, like restitution."

"That's a biggie. Why now?"

"Adam went to talk with Greg, who has taken over management of the account. Apparently, Greg was evasive about how River City had lost so much money from the pension fund. He denied any knowledge of offshore accounts even though Adam had gotten wind of Greg's wife's comments at the gala a few weeks back."

"It's a small town. Word like that gets around quickly."

"Twice as quickly at the mill. Anyway, Rob said they argued and had words. Adam is calling a special meeting of the union right away to ask for a vote of some kind. I guess it would be to authorize a lawsuit."

"I didn't think this mess could get any messier, but clearly I was wrong."

"Speaking of the mess, are you any closer to helping Nolan solve the case? Are they calling it a murder officially?"

"Not really. Suspicious death is more accurate. Every time I think I've come up with the explanation I find another bunny trail. And it's not even close to Easter."

Carly laughed. "Good luck. My vote's on you for figuring it out."

"I'm not sure Nolan and Kilkelly would agree with you right now. Anyway, tell Rob I said hi and thanks for the update on the pension case."

JULIA CALLED Nolan on the pretense of telling him what she'd learned about Greg and Adam's conversation, although she really wanted to know about his conversation with Greg at the bank.

She related what she'd just learned from Carly about the union's plans to sue River City Bank.

"That's interesting," said Nolan. "Because Greg told me he had talked to Drake a couple of weeks ago about switching to Parkview National Bank. He'd said he was disappointed in how Jay was managing the bank, although he didn't mention the ESCO account specifically."

"I wonder if that's why Sandra Lantz and Becca Morrison

sounded so chummy when I overheard them in the ladies' room."

"That would make sense. He told me that he'd stopped by Jay's house the Friday evening before the gala to have a friendly chat."

"Did they drink grog?"

"No, but they did have a shot or two of scotch, which would explain that second glass in the sink."

"I get the impression you don't peg him as trying to get back at Jay."

"No, I don't. Greg had more to gain by moving to the other bank and maybe taking the ESCO account with him."

"Hm. So it's more likely that Jay would be angry with Greg than the other way around," said Julia. "What time was he there? Could Jay have had another visitor that evening?"

"Greg said he was there about six thirty, so there was plenty of time for someone else to stop by."

"Yeah. Someone with grog. Did you get that list of owners from MacGroggery Distillery yet?"

"They emailed it but I haven't looked at it yet."

"May I see it?

"I'll forward it when I get a chance."

"One more thing...what about the gun in Jay's file cabinet? Did you find any history on that?"

"Sorry...forgot to tell you what I learned. It's registered to Jay in the State of Connecticut. There was no record of it having been used in any crimes so for now it's just a detail, not a clue."

"And you still haven't found the laptop, right?"

"Correct. Kilkelly is getting ready to declare this as an unsolved but suspicious death. There's just no direction to go with the little we have, Aunt Julia."

"I know. Oh, well. It took thirty years or so to solve the Green River murders in King County so there's always hope that justice will prevail."

Nolan chuckled. "The perennial optimist!"

CHAPTER 21
MYSTERY MONEY

J ulia read the names of the investors in the distillery as soon as she opened the email at home. She didn't know all of them, mostly men, but recognized a handful of names—Drake Ashford, Jay Morrison and a few other locals, in addition to the members of the country club golf group. She paused when she read the name *Giblewison Enterprises*. It was the only entity that was listed as a company instead of an individual. *What an odd name for a company,* she thought to herself. Nothing else was a surprise. She was sure Nolan would notice that Drake's name was on the list and guessed he would call on him and check his house for a bottle of grog, hopefully tainted with the methanol. She decided to ask him about it at the next opportunity.

Since she already had her laptop booted up, she Googled the addresses on the envelopes to Melissa LeAnne Carlton that had been in the probate documents. The first address was in the Green Lake neighborhood, but the house would have been in the middle of the lake if it were an actual residence. The second of the two was on Capitol Hill, right in the center of

Volunteer Park. Julia smiled at the cleverness, or boldness, of whoever had come up with the fake places. She scanned copies for Nolan and sent them by email with a comment of her own. "Lake property for sale in Seattle. Enjoy a view of Green Lake." She added a happy face.

She made a list of to-dos for Thursday. Calling MacGroggery Distillery and dropping in on Angela at the River City Bank were at the top of the list. She sensed that she was getting closer to the truth, both regarding the mystery of the methanol source and discovering who supposedly killed LeAnne. She shivered in her chair in front of the fireplace despite being wrapped in a fuzzy blanket.

THE EARLY MORNING minutes dragged by. Julia did low-impact aerobics while watching a favorite DVD as she waited to call Angela at eight thirty, when the bank opened. She secured an appointment for one o'clock and promised to invite Nolan and Kilkelly to be there if one or both were available.

Nolan didn't answer his phone so Julia left him a quick message to call when he was free. She considered the possibility that he might be talking with Drake and could give her an update. If that were the case it would be a two-for-one call.

Though MacGroggery Distillery's website listed only the hours for tours and tastings, Julia figured they had to be on the premises doing something during the morning hours, like making their products. A polite woman with a low-pitched voice answered the phone. When Julia explained the reason for the call, she was transferred to the business office. Julia heard metal clinks and loud thuds in the background as she waited for someone to pick up the call. It sounded like she was on an open line in the warehouse-like building.

"Bryce MacGregor," a male voice said. "How can I help you?"

After identifying herself, Julia told him about Nolan having shared the investors list with her. She hoped he recalled meeting her the weekend before. Men often remembered her adorable sister, so she added that detail as well. When he acknowledged having seen them in the tasting room, she asked him about the entity listed as Giblewison Enterprises. He was reluctant to reveal any information initially but relented when Julia implied that the deputy sheriff and Detective Kilkelly could make a second visit.

"That was a funny deal. It was two guys who had a pile of money that they said was from winning big at the casino down the freeway. My gut said they weren't telling the truth, but I don't really care how people get their money. I'm glad to take it off their hands." He laughed, although the tone of his voice lacked humor.

"Do they have real names?"

"They kept telling me to use their business name, that Gibble-something. I never heard them say it out loud, only saw it in writing."

"Do you have any idea who they are?" Julia wished she had Carly's charm. She surely could get the names from Bryce.

"No, I don't, but I heard the shorter one call the other guy Peter."

JULIA DISSECTED the business name into syllables—Gib-Lew-is-son. Could it be Gibson and Lewis? Alex and Peter? She smacked her fist on the kitchen counter where she was sitting on a tall stool as she rehydrated herself. Why make up such a name? Are they hiding something? Where did the money come from? Alex didn't seem like a gambler to her.

Nolan called shortly before twelve. "I don't think Drake's our guy. We searched the house and didn't find anything helpful. He didn't have Jay's laptop, but he had a bottle of that MacGrog all right. But it was sealed. He said it was a gift for being one of the investors."

Julia listened impatiently. "Yes, I agree with you."

"You do?"

She told him what she'd learned from Bryce MacGregor. "Mr. MacGregor said he didn't know the men's actual names but I'm sure it's Peter and Alex. They and Jay have all known each other since living in Hartford before they moved here."

"Not so fast, Aunt Julia. I need something else."

"Okay. One of them may well be the purveyor of the Friday night grog and the other one an abettor. Can't you at least go to their homes and search for a bottle of grog?"

"I'm not going to be able to get a search warrant based on that. I need solid information."

Julia sighed. "I'll put on my thinking hat. What about this afternoon's appointment with Angela at River City? Will you be there? Maybe she'll have that solid information."

"That I can do. We'll see you there."

"It turns out the money went to an offshore account. It wasn't easy to persuade the investigation team to look into it even when I told them how much money was in it," said Angela. "When I mentioned it might be related to the death of the account's owner, they agreed to act sooner instead of later." Angela invited her three guests to stand behind her chair so she could share her screen with them.

"As I mentioned when we talked earlier, this account is in the name of Jay Morrison. There's no other name on record although accounts like this often have silent or invisible co-owners who are identified in other documents. I wasn't given that information."

Angela pointed out the deposits that had been made since the account had been opened. For the first several years, the dollar amounts were mostly five figures, occasionally six. They seemed to occur in a random pattern for the first five years. Then there was a deposit of just over fifteen million dollars five years earlier. No deposits were made for three more years. Then a deposit of one hundred fifty thousand dollars was documented, followed by two more similar deposits six and twelve months later.

"Those might be the ESCO money," Julia said as Nolan nodded. "Angela, is there a way to trace those last three deposits back to this bank?"

"It's already been done. I've talked with the suits about the legal process we need to go through to get it back. With interest, I might add." She smiled as she sat back.

"That's going to make the union guys very happy," said Julia. "And Drake, too, probably. His bank will likely get the account back with this information."

"That's all I have for now on that, but I've been able to unravel some information from the other statements you gave me, Julia."

"You mean Ms. Carlton's account?"

"Yes. Another interesting sequence of events. Go ahead and have a seat." She indicated the chairs on the other side of her desk. "This one's more straightforward."

"I'm guessing Jay is involved again," said Julia.

"Good guess." Angela smiled. "Once the senior Mr. Morrison died, Jay was given access to his father's accounts. I'm assuming he noticed the regular payment that was going to Ms. Carlton's account. He probably did a little investigating to see what it was for, and subsequently stopped the electronic transactions a couple of months later."

"And closed the account?" said Julia.

"Well, I would have expected that to happen, but Jay's name was on it as well so he kept it open instead. He's been making periodic deposits as well as executing a few withdrawals."

"Is Becca's name on the account?"

"That's odd, too, but no. It's only in Jay's name officially. But there is another signer on the account."

"Can you tell us who it is?" asked Nolan.

"Peter Lewis."

"How much money are you talking about," asked Kilkelly.

"Just over five million dollars."

CHAPTER 22
TECHNICAL KNOCKOUT

LeAnne was at the nurse's station when Julia stopped by. LeAnne greeted her with, "Hi! You're smiling like that proverbial Cheshire Cat. What do you know?"

"I'd love to meet you at Grant's when you're done with your shift today. This might be the day we get to celebrate."

"And you're not going to tell me anything else, are you?"

"No," Julia admitted. "There are a few more steps that have to be taken before I can do that. See you there about four-ish?"

JULIA HUMMED the tune to an old song, *I Heard it Through the Grape Vine*, as she drove through the tree-lined streets to her home. Ellie waved from her yard where she was planting a small shrub in an empty spot near the front entrance. Julia nodded her approval as she turned into her driveway. She saw Trixie through the French door at the side entrance, tapping her front feet and barking a greeting. Julia turned the key and entered, then reached for the control panel to disable the alarm system. As she reminded her dog to stop barking, she realized the alarm hadn't beeped its usual signal that it had been disarmed. *Maybe I forgot to set it this morning.* She knelt to scratch Trixie behind the ears, then heard rustling behind her. She turned and saw a figure in black as it rushed forward. Julia opened her mouth to scream. A wet spray hit her face. She gasped, tried to spit out the bitter substance, closed her eyes, and turned away. A sharp pain shot through the back of her head and she fell to the floor.

LeAnne checked her watch for the third time. Julia was twenty minutes late. *Maybe she got sidetracked. Maybe she meant tomorrow instead of today. No, she meant today and she specified Grant's. So where is she?* LeAnne shook her head, puzzled. She checked her phone for new messages but saw none. Getting worried given the recent events, she dialed Julia's phone but got her voicemail. She left a message that she would swing by Julia's house instead of waiting any longer.

Grateful that Julia had shared her contact file with her, she set her car's GPS and pulled up in front of the house ten minutes later. She saw Julia's Infiniti parked in the driveway and hurried toward the front door.

LeAnne rang the bell and heard the ding-dong, but Julia didn't come to the door. She heard barking from farther inside. She tried the bell again, waited a moment, but still no answer.

She heard someone call out and turned to see a woman waving at her from across the street.

"She should be inside if you're looking for Julia. I'm her neighbor, Ellie."

"Hi. I'm LeAnne, one of the nurses at the hospital. I tried calling but she didn't answer her phone."

"I heard her dog barking earlier but otherwise I haven't heard anything. There's a side entrance. That's how she usually goes in," said Ellie as she walked across the street to join LeAnne. "It's around this way." She was poised to knock when she looked through the glass door and saw Julia on the floor with a pool of blood next to her head. She screamed.

LeAnne tossed her cell phone to Ellie. "Call 911! Tell them to send an ambulance and the police." She pushed the unlocked door open. LeAnne knelt beside her friend and quickly did an assessment as per her training. Julia was breathing and had a pulse. It was regular but faint. Julia groaned and tried to sit up when LeAnne checked her head wound, which was oozing blood. It was a couple of centimeters long and would require sutures. LeAnne gently but firmly told her to lie still. She didn't see any other external injuries. Ellie found a thin pillow and set it on the floor next to her friend. Once LeAnne was certain Julia's neck was stable, she slid the pillow under her head. Sirens blared down the street. Ellie hurried outside to direct the emergency medical personnel to the sunroom.

LeAnne gave the lead EMT a brief assessment and stepped aside. She watched as they hooked Julia up to a portable electrocardiogram, measured her blood pressure and pulse, checked her for other external injuries, and started an IV line.

Julia opened her eyes when she was being lifted onto the gurney and saw LeAnne. "Did I miss our celebration?"

DETECTIVE KILKELLY and Officer Mealy arrived within another minute and checked the interior of the house for any intruders in case they were still in the house. The house alarm system was disarmed, according to the panel. The back door was closed but an adjacent utility room window was open. Kilkelly directed two other newly arrived officers to gather forensic evidence.

LeAnne and Ellie gave the police their individual accounts of what had happened.

Ellie denied seeing any other car or strangers during the time she had been working in her yard. "But someone could have entered her yard from the alley and gone in the back way. I can't see that from here." She sniffled into a tissue.

"My officers will survey the neighbors." Kilkelly asked Ellie, "Did you hear the alarm go off?"

"No. All I heard was Trixie, her dog, barking some when Julia came home about an hour ago, but that's not unusual."

"Do you know if she always set her alarm when she was out of the house?"

"We've never talked about it. I don't know."

Kilkelly turned to LeAnne. "Ms. Carlton, do you happen to know if she always uses her alarm system?"

LeAnne shook her head. "This is my first time here. We've never talked about her house alarm. I know *I* would set it, but she might not worry about it in the daylight hours."

"Do either of you know what someone might be looking for inside? Has she said anything that she's worried about?" asked Kilkelly.

LeAnne said, "I think you know she's been helping me try to recover part of my inheritance from Jay Morrison's estate, but I don't know if she had anything at her home that would be worth breaking in for."

"Yes, I'm aware of your situation."

Ellie said, "I don't know anything about valuables she might have but there was somebody lurking around her house after dark about a week ago. I'm not sure if she reported it, though."

"She might have told Nolan. I'll check. That's all I need for now. Thank you for your help, ladies. Officer Mealy and I will verify the doors are locked as we leave. I'll talk with Dr.

Fairchild at the hospital when she's stable." Kilkelly gave each of the two women a business card. "Call me if you think of anything. And I mean *anything.*"

"I'm going to the hospital and check on her," LeAnne said to Ellie.

"Please let me know what you find out," said Ellie.

CHAPTER 23
FOR THE LOVE OF MONEY

Julia joked with the nurses and Dr. Gorman as the emergency department physician finished closing her scalp laceration with one last suture.

"Done," he pronounced. "Okay, Julia. I know you're a doctor yourself but please let one of your partners take these sutures out. I want them to see my handiwork." He winked at her.

"Of course," she said, laughing. "I'll get more sympathy that way. May I leave now?"

"In a few minutes. I need to verify that the CT was negative for brain contusion or skull fracture. And there are a couple of police-type people who want to talk with you before I let you go. And you'll need a driver to take you home. No driving for twenty-four hours."

"I could walk to work from my house."

LeAnne spoke up. "No, you're not going to do that. I called your office already and they've cleared your schedule. I hope that was all right. And I'll take you home today. I owe you that."

"Thank you, LeAnne. I suppose I could use a day off."

Despite Julia's protests, the emergency room nurse insisted that she ride in a wheelchair to the interview room where Kilkelly and Mealy were waiting.

Julia told the officers what had happened when she had gone home earlier. She admitted that she wasn't sure if she had set her alarm earlier, although she usually did when she was gone all day for work.

"It looks like they gained access through a window in your utility room. Did you know you have a broken latch?" Officer Mealy asked.

Julia groaned. "I totally forgot to get the latch fixed on that window. I don't think about it except when I'm in there doing laundry and I forget by the time I leave the room."

"Obviously, you should get it fixed right away. Does anyone else have a key to your house?" asked Kilkelly.

"My sister Carly has one, but I can't imagine her giving it to anyone else, and she would tell me if she did."

"Anyone else? A housekeeper? A pet sitter?"

"I don't have a housekeeper, but my friend, Pam, watches Trixie for me when I'm out of town. She has one."

"Can you please call her to see if she's loaned it out?"

"Sure." Julia reached for her purse and sighed. "I don't have my cell phone on me. Can I call her from home?"

"Yes, and let me know right away what she says," said Kilkelly. "That's all for now. I trust Ms. Carlton to get you home. I'll let you know if I learn anything else." The officers excused themselves.

LeAnne followed, pushing Julia in the wheelchair, while Kilkelly held the door open. "Okay, Julia. Let's get you home. I hope you didn't have any hot dates tonight."

"We still need to have a little celebration."

"No wine for you tonight. Doctor's orders. But I'll let you

tell me what we would have been celebrating when I get you squared away."

LeAnne puttered around Julia's den and found a blanket to tuck around her friend where she sat on the loveseat. She started the gas fire with a flick of a switch and prepared a couple of mugs of hot chocolate. Julia whined at being treated like an invalid, but LeAnne shushed her and pointed to her own head as a reminder to Julia.

LeAnne pulled Julia's leather chair closer to the loveseat and sat down. "Now I'd like to hear what you were so excited about earlier."

Julia shared what she and the officers had learned about the offshore accounts. LeAnne whistled when she heard the size of the balance.

"A good share of that money is almost certainly from your father's estate," said Julia. "The fifteen-million-dollar deposit five or six years ago corresponds to when he died."

"And you think that Becca doesn't know about that account?"

"She may know about the bank but not necessarily about that particular deposit. Jay seemed to be sneaky. And there's more." Julia slurped her chocolate. "Too bad I can't open a bottle of Prosecco for you."

"Julia..." LeAnne scolded.

"Kidding. We can have some another day."

"Tell me about the 'there's more' part."

"Angela—she works at River City Bank—traced the monthly deposits into your mom's account to a bank in Bellevue. The account had belonged to your father. No surprise there. Jay inherited it after his dad died. What *is* a surprise is that after stopping the money transfers to your mom, he kept it open. I have a hunch that Becca doesn't know it exists."

"She'll want a part of that, I'm sure, once she hears about it."

"Probably. Jay has made some deposits and withdrawals during the last several years but it still has a balance of over five million dollars."

"No way!"

"Yes. I wonder if your father was ensuring there would be enough money in the account to take care of you and your mom for many years."

LeAnne sat back in her chair. "Wow."

"And there's more."

"More money?"

Julia shook her head. "Peter Lewis, Jay's attorney, is a co-signer on the account.'"

"Instead of Becca?"

Julia arched an eyebrow. "That's the same reaction I had."

LeAnne finished her cocoa as Carly arrived to spend the night at Julia's house. Julia tried to protest but LeAnne was firm. "You need a responsible person present in case your headache worsens or you start vomiting. I've leaving Carly in charge. I'll call to check on you in the morning." She kissed her friend on the forehead and said, "Be good."

Julia made a face at LeAnne before telling Carly where she would find an icepack (in the freezer) and the ibuprofen (in the corner drawer next to the kitchen sink).

"Have you talked to Alex yet?" Carly sank into Julia's favorite chair after refilling the mugs of hot chocolate.

"No. I'm going to wait until Nolan and Kilkelly have talked with Peter Lewis."

"Huh? What does that have to do with talking to Alex?"

"Maybe nothing, but they *are* partners, and I don't want to say anything that might get back to Peter."

"I'm not following you at all, sister."

Julia gave Carly a Cliff's Notes version of Angela's report and what she had learned at the distillery that morning.

"Oh—Gib-lewis-son. I get it now." Carly stared at the fire for a long moment. "And you're dating Alex. I get it, but I can't imagine him trying to break into your house. What would he, or whoever, be looking for? Your laptop, maybe?"

Julia shook her head and pointed to her left. "It's sitting right there on the table and so is the folder with the printouts of senior Mr. Morrison's will and other stuff. Most of the actual incriminating evidence is at the bank, not here."

"Maybe it's just a tactic to scare you off the trail."

"It's too late for that. Kilkelly knows everything I know. *He's* not going to stop checking things out."

"Same with Nolan. He's got the Finnish *sisu* like you and me." Carly saluted with her mug.

Julia awoke the next morning with a throbbing headache. She padded into the den and curled up with a blanket. Her sister promptly produced a fresh ice pack and two ibuprofen tablets, then checked the bandage and the incision. "There's a little dried blood but it looks good. I think you can go without a bandage today."

"I would love to wash my hair. It feels so grody!" Julia patted her blood-matted hair and scowled. "I know I can't get the wound wet for the first twenty-four hours, but I have some dry shampoo in the bathroom. At least it would feel cleaner."

"I can help you with that after your shower."

Freshly bathed, Julia sat in a kitchen chair with a towel

around her shoulders while Carly gently cleaned her hair. "I haven't used this stuff in years. I guess it just absorbs oil because I don't see how it cleans anything. I'll use this rubbing alcohol on the dried blood." She dabbed the wound while Julia winced at the sting.

"Ouch!"

"Sorry. This blood is stuck to your scalp and it's hard to get it loose. You'd better wear a hat when you go out for a day or two."

"Good idea. It's going to be cold enough to get away with wearing a knit cap. Nobody will know I'm really in camouflage."

Carly laughed at her older sister. "Only you would think of something like that."

"Thanks for doing my hair. Hey...that reminds me. I'm supposed to ask you and Pam about my house key. You haven't loaned it to anyone. Right?"

"Of course not. And I can't imagine Pam giving it out, either. Do you want me to ask her when I get to work? I can swing by her office in the next building. I already told my boss I would be a couple of hours late. If you think you're going to be okay by yourself, that is."

"I'll be fine. Ellie will be looking in on me." Julia glanced at the time. "Pam should be at her desk by now. Where's my cell phone?" After telling Pam about the break-in at her house and her injury, she asked about the key. "No, I didn't expect that you would loan it to anyone else, but I swore to that detective I would ask. Just keeping my promise." She smiled as she heard Pam's concern. "Thanks. Carly came over last night but I'm okay now. Let's get together tomorrow." Julia nodded at her friend's suggestion. "Perfect. Bye."

"What did you agree to?"

"She wants to meet me at The Silver Door when I feel up to

it. She's redoing her kitchen and wants some help with colors and all that."

"That sounds safe enough. I'll come to check on you tomorrow morning." Carly put the breakfast dishes in the dishwasher, poured Julia a second cup of coffee, and locked the door behind her as she left.

JULIA CURLED up in her big chair with her mug, cell phone at hand. LeAnne and her medical assistant, Amie, each checked up on her by phone during the next half-hour. At ten, Ellie tapped on the side door, which sent Trixie into a happy dance. She loved company.

"I intercepted the delivery guy so I could claim I got you these flowers." Ellie carried a beautiful bouquet of flowers. "Aren't these pretty?" she asked as she placed them on Julia's mantel. "The card says 'Get well. Love, Alex.'"

Julia frowned. "How does he know? I didn't talk to him."

Ellie shrugged. "They're gorgeous. Just enjoy them."

"I will. There's coffee in the kitchen. It's probably still warm."

"Did you and the police come up with any explanation for the break-in?"

"No. I didn't find anything missing. Not like at Jay's house, where some files had been taken." She waved at the table with the laptop and file folder.

Ellie looked at the table and nodded, then frowned. "This folder looks pretty thin." She picked it up and opened it. "It's empty."

CHAPTER 24

GHOSTS OF BROTHERHOOD

"We really need to quit meeting like this," Julia said when she met Nolan at the door. She gave him a summary of the contents of the now-empty folder. It had contained the probated will of Jay's father, the River City bank's ESCO statements, and pertinent notes she had written as she uncovered details and bits of information.

"So whoever took the file knows pretty much everything you've discovered," said Nolan.

"Except what's in my head that I didn't write down."

"Like what?"

"I didn't get a chance to jot down anything from our visit yesterday with Angela. Like finding out the co-signer on his father's old account is Peter. And figuring out the translation of *Giblewison* represents Peter and Alex. Or that I've seen the dark Camry with the pink decal. Twice."

Nolan nodded. "We may still have some advantage then. I already have copies of the documents you mentioned. Is there anything else you think might be helpful to us?"

Julia scrolled through the documents in the e-file folder

she had labeled MLC—Melissa LeAnne Carlton. She printed a page and handed it to Nolan. "This is LeAnne's mother's address and phone number. Her address was on those bank statements. I would feel better if you had someone in Seattle check on her. Just in case."

"I'll contact the Seattle Police Department. Anything else?"

"What about talking with Peter Lewis and Alex Gibson about their investment at the distillery?"

"Kilkelly and I discussed that, and we decided we don't have enough information to link them to Jay's death. It's not illegal to form a company for investing."

"Another good lead down the drain," said Julia.

"We need something more than that to make a move," Nolan said as he took his leave.

He was halfway down the sidewalk when Julia's cell rang.

"You're not going to believe this one," said Carly. "I saw a dark gray Camry with a breast cancer decal parked in our employee lot when I pulled in. I took a picture that I'll send you by text."

"Thanks. Nolan is just leaving. I'll tell him."

Julia yelled at Nolan as he was climbing into his patrol unit SUV and motioned for him to come back. Julia's phone pinged with the promised message. She showed the photo of the license plate and the car to Nolan. "Carly said it's sitting in the ESCO parking lot nearest the accounting office."

"Maybe this is the break we've been waiting for," he said as he trotted back to his rig.

JULIA SWALLOWED two more ibuprofens and curled up on her loveseat while she waited for them to take effect. She noticed the vase of flowers on the mantel and realized she hadn't called Alex yet to thank him.

"Hi, Beautiful. Are you feeling okay?"

"A little better. I'm lying on the couch admiring the beautiful yellow roses and baby's breath in the bouquet that was delivered this morning. I was surprised that you already knew about my incident."

"Peter told me. I'm not sure how he knew. I was so shook up I didn't even ask."

"So much for confidentiality laws," said Julia, thinking *How did Peter know?*

"Have the police figured out a motive yet?"

"No. I probably just interrupted a burglar before he found anything to take. My laptop was in plain sight and there's not much else of value in here anyway."

"Are you sure it was a burglar? You got shot at last week and now you've been whacked on the head. Maybe you should turn in your detective badge and leave the sleuthing up to the experts."

Julia started to ask him how he knew she'd been whacked on the head because that detail hadn't been revealed as far as she knew. She had told the emergency triage nurse that she hit her head on a coffee table. She felt a chill run up her spine. "I know we had dinner plans for tonight but I'm not going to be good company. How about we skip it and have our regular Mexican dinner on Sunday instead?"

"Okay. I'll have dinner and Friday night drinks with a couple of the guys at the country club."

"Sounds like a good idea. Thanks again for the flowers."

Julia cradled her phone for a moment. *How did Peter know she'd been hit on the head? Who told him? And what else did he know?* Julia mulled over the unanswered thoughts.

. . .

CARLY HAD a good view of the parking area from her second-floor office window. She glanced at the Camry every few minutes as if she could mentally command it to stay there until Nolan showed up. After about fifteen minutes she saw that it was backing up. She'd missed seeing who got into the driver's seat. Several more minutes passed before she saw a patrol car pull into that same spot. She watched Nolan and Officer Mealy walk around the lot looking for the Camry. They had apparently missed seeing it as they drove into the parking lot. She left her desk and hurried down to meet them.

"Hi, Aunt Carly," said Nolan. "Have you met Officer Mealy?"

They nodded at each other and shook hands. "The car left about five or six minutes ago. I wasn't looking when the driver got in so I can't help you there."

"I ran the plates, thanks to your cleverness in taking the picture, so we can identify the owner."

"But that doesn't mean it's the same person driving it."

"True. We'll give them a call and go from there." Seeing Carly's sad face, he added, "We're closing in on somebody. Thanks to observant people like you."

She nodded glumly. "I'm worried about Julia. She's already been seriously injured. I mean, she could have been killed! And she won't listen to reason and back off. Maybe she'll listen to you if you tell her to stick to practicing medicine and leave the detecting to you."

Officer Mealy nodded. "You have a legitimate concern but you know how stubborn she is and probably won't listen to Nolan or me either. We've beefed up the patrol rounds of her neighborhood. We aim to keep her safe." He smiled and tipped his hat.

· · ·

JULIA BOOTED up her laptop and printed the scans of the original documents that had been stolen the previous day. She found a spiral-bound notebook and wrote down all the additional details that she could remember. *Somewhere in here is a clue to solving the puzzle,* Julia thought. She listed the pertinent events as she understood them in chronological order, beginning with Jay's birth, then LeAnne's birth, Jay's work history, his father's death, and so on.

She puzzled over the fact that Jay, Peter and Alex all had been connected to Globisphere in some way and that they all had ended up in Parkview. Was Globisphere the connection? Or was it something else? Who else knew about Jay siphoning money from his employer? Had anyone other than Peter known about the offshore accounts until Greg stumbled onto them? Could one of them have been blackmailing Jay? If so, who was it? Or did Jay have something on one of the other two?

The church bells chimed three. Julia's twenty-four hours of no driving and no alcohol were up. She padded into the kitchen and poured herself a glass of cabernet using one of the Waterford wine glasses that a friend had convinced her to buy at an outlet store. Inexpensive wine tasted better that way, she told herself.

Back at her makeshift workstation, she wondered if Becca or LeAnne were as innocent as Julia had assumed. There was a fortune in money at stake. LeAnne appeared to have a legitimate claim for a large chunk of money. Did Becca make a move to keep more of it for herself? Did the two of them work together when Jay refused to share? But how would they have known each other if that were the case?

Nolan called to tell her that the Camry parked at ESCO belonged to Adam Johns' wife, Linda, and that he had been driving it while his own rig was in the shop. Being a big guy and in the union as well, he was sensitive about the pink breast cancer sticker, Nolan added. "I'm pretty sure this isn't the car you saw at Jay's house. We'll keep looking. I promise."

Julia reminded herself that not everything that had happened in the past two weeks was necessarily related to Jay. Or LeAnne. Even if it all seemed to be intertwined.

CHAPTER 25

TRUTH OR CONSEQUENCES?

J ulia heard Trixie's happy, tapping feet hurry to the side door. She looked over her shoulder to see LeAnne waiting outside with a big smile while holding a potted orchid and a bottle of wine. Julia jumped up to greet her.

"What a pleasant surprise!" said Julia. "Thank you for coming over."

"I thought you might need a nurse to check on you." She set the plant next to the floral arrangement from Alex. She glanced at the gift tag. "From Alex?"

Julia nodded. "He said he found out from Peter. News travels fast."

"It looks like you already have a glass of wine poured. May I join you? We can drink this other bottle another time when we're truly celebrating."

Julia widened her eyes when she saw that the wine was a Chateau Ste. Michelle cabernet sauvignon reserve. "I'll say."

They sat on the loveseat with their glasses of wine. Julia shared her earlier musings, ending with the question in her mind about whether Becca had played a role.

LeAnne shook her head. "I don't see it. She's a mom and I don't think she'd risk losing those boys for this. Even if it is a lot of money."

"I want to agree with you. Given Jay's reckless habits, she'd end up with the money sooner or later."

"More likely sooner from what I know."

"I'm not ready to exclude Greg Lantz yet," said Julia. "He had a lot to gain with Jay gone and might have worried about Jay retaliating over those offshore accounts."

"Didn't you say something about his approaching Drake to discuss changing banks? Maybe he had words with Jay and decided he'd had enough."

"Plausible." Julia pulled a blanket around her shoulders. "I keep having this inkling that Alex knows something about it."

"What kind of inkling?"

Julia pursed her lips. "Earlier today when I called him to thank him for the flowers he made a comment about my having been whacked on the head. How would he know that? I told Dr. Gorman in the ED that I hit my head on the coffee table. Only you, Nolan and Mealy, and the emergency personnel know otherwise."

"Hm. That *is* curious. Unless he has ESP."

LeAnne checked Julia's head wound and gave her permission to wash her hair in the morning.

"Hallelujah!"

"I'm free tomorrow morning so I'll stop by and check on you before I head north to see my mom."

"Thanks. You're a gem."

JULIA FORTIFIED HERSELF WITH IBUPROFEN, topped off her wine, grabbed a blanket, and started the fire. She curled up on the loveseat with her current book, another murder mystery. She had started the third chapter when her front doorbell rang. Out of habit she noted the time. It was just after eight p.m., not a normal time for drop-in visitors. She followed her dog, Trixie's tail a-wagging, to the door and peeked through the old-fashioned peephole, a tiny door on the inside which covered a miniature window at eye level.

Julia quickly checked her appearance in the foyer mirror and fluffed her hair before unlocking and opening the door. "Alex. What brings you here?"

Alex wobbled a little as he stepped inside. "Sorry it's late. I have something to confess to you. I didn't want to tell you over the phone."

"Join me in the den. I'm going to get you a glass of water if you don't mind."

"Oh, sure. I had enough to drink at the club." He walked unsteadily to the chair and sat down, waiting for Julia to join him.

She handed him a glass of water and started to pick up her own glass of wine but thought better of it. Finishing her wine could wait. "What do you need to tell me?"

"It's about Jay. I have an idea about what might have happened." He held his eyes on Julia for a moment then looked away.

"I'm happy to listen."

"You know I'm the executor of his will. We'd had a few talks lately after his half-sister showed up a few months ago. He started having second thoughts about what had happened when his father died."

"You mean the forged death certificate?"

"Yes, so you know about that?"

"I do. So does the police detective. And his sister."

"Okay. Well, he had been raised thinking he was an only child and when he saw that will of his dad's, he kinda freaked out. He felt entitled, I think, and couldn't fathom having to share any of the estate with this unknown person. He told me he went to Peter's law firm, and they helped him with the death certificate and all."

"So he truly didn't know about the sister until his father died?"

Alex shook his head. "I guess his dad never told his mom. He kept a secret bank account that Jay inherited and that's how he found out about the payments—guilt payments, in a way—to the mistress."

Julia smiled kindly. "Or love payments."

Alex looked up with a thin smile. "I suppose."

"What do you think happened?" Julia took a swallow of her wine, after all.

"Once Melissa—or LeAnne as she goes by—contacted Jay a few months ago, he started to feel guilty about what he'd done. She's his only living relative other than his two boys and he told Peter he wanted to come clean about what he'd done five or six years ago."

"Did he talk about making restitution with his sister?"

"Yeah, in some way or another."

"Then what happened?"

"Peter tried to dissuade him, but Jay was determined to go through with it. He asked me for a recommendation for legal assistance because Peter refused to go along with it. Being Peter's partner, there was nothing I could do but recommend another attorney for Jay."

"Why?"

"Peter was worried that he would be found to have helped Jay provide the false death certificate. Which might lead to discovery that he had also helped conceal some of Jay's assets. He had been listed as a signer on his offshore accounts. That's one of the details that Greg Lantz had stumbled onto."

"Do you know which attorney he talked to?"

"Probably no one. Our conversation was on Thursday, just before the big gala, and then he died the day after that." He reached for Julia's glass and took a swallow. "I'm worried Peter had something to do with it."

Julia reached over to Alex and cradled him as he started sobbing. "I'll call the detective and you can tell him with me here."

CHAPTER 26

THE LAST LOOSE END

Julia, Carly and LeAnne were enjoying a cappuccino on Saturday morning when Nolan and Kilkelly stopped by.

"Alex's hunch about Peter was right on the money— no pun intended," said Nolan, chuckling at his own joke. "We found an open bottle of MacGrog in the back of his liquor cabinet. It smelled odd. Might have some methanol in it."

"I think he would have added methanol to Jay's glass and not to the bottle," said Julia. "He wouldn't have risked drinking it himself."

"He could have poured the rest of the methanol into the bottle afterwards. That could explain it if he didn't want to have a partial bottle of methanol lying around. We'll know soon. Anyway, we found a briefcase with Jay's initials on it and a laptop inside. Funny thing, the briefcase looked old and used."

"Maybe it was our father's. They had the same initials— WJM," said LeAnne. She laughed. "It feels weird to think of Will that way. He was only a name before but now he's starting to feel like a real person. The dad I never got to know." She sighed.

Nolan nodded. "We'll have our experts have a go at the laptop and see what he's hiding there, if anything. Thanks to Angela and Julia, we have a handle on some of his other holdings. Mr. Lewis isn't being very cooperative yet. He wants a lawyer, of course." Nolan snorted.

"He'll need one," said Kilkelly. "A really good one."

"What about the gunshots? Did he confess to those?" asked Julia.

Kilkelly chuckled. "Before Peter could stop her, his girlfriend, who rushed up when we first questioned him, said he bribed her younger brother to drive by on his motorcycle to try to scare you and Drake."

"I'll bet she won't be his girlfriend much longer," said Carly.

"Does anyone want to know what we found out about the Camry with the pink decal?" asked Kilkelly.

Julia raised her hand. "I'd love to know who it belongs to."

"It was parked in Peter's driveway when we got there. His girlfriend said it was her mom's car and that she had lived in Florida before moving here. It turns out the pink decal was a flamingo, after all. Good eye, Julia!"

Julia pumped her arm and squealed. "Yes!"

"That's about it," said Nolan.

"I called Sophia after you all left last night," said Julia. "I told her you had pretty much solved the case. She's glad about that and said she and the baby are doing fine. If she has a boy, she's thinking of naming him Nolan." Julia winked at her nephew, whose face started turning beet red.

The doorbell sounded; Trixie scampered to the side door where Alex waited. Julia waved an invitation to come in and greeted him with a brief hug.

"May I join you? It looks like you're having a little party."

"I suppose it is kind of a party. Come on in and meet LeAnne," said Julia. She introduced Alex and LeAnne to each other, then stepped aside.

"Thank you for helping with the final puzzle piece," said LeAnne. "I'm sorry I never got to meet my brother in person but it sounds like he might have been a decent guy, after all."

"He had some good moments. I'm sure he would tell me that I should help you any way I can, so please let me know when you need me."

LeAnne stepped forward and gave him a big hug. "I might just do that."

It was almost noon before Julia's house was empty of all the extra company. LeAnne headed to Seattle with a promise from Nolan that he would be sure she got the briefcase when forensics was done with it. Carly left to go to her beach house with her husband on his rare weekend off work. Alex had a tee time at the club with his foursome. Nolan and Kilkelly went back to work.

Julia curled up on her loveseat with Trixie at her side. Normally she wouldn't allow her dog on the furniture—she had plenty of dog beds to choose from. Julia used the remote switch to play one of her favorite musical CDs on her new-but-looks-vintage multi-use player. The orchestral overture from *Phantom of the Opera* filled the room. She was taken back to the theatre where she'd seen it performed on stage four or five times. She'd lost track. She pictured Christine sitting at her vanity while the invisible Angel of Music sang to her.

She reflected on what she had learned about Alex over the course of the last few days. He hadn't been forthright about a number of things involving Jay and his past, and that bothered her. She was disappointed to learn that he'd played a role in Jay's inheritance cover-up, whether innocently or not. She wondered if he ever would have told her had he not been drunk enough to feel remorseful. He had broken her trust in his integrity and she knew she wouldn't be seeing him anymore except at social events.

Julia sighed and took another swallow of wine. Would she ever meet anyone with whom she could have a satisfying, honest relationship?

"At least I've got you, Trixie. You've never lied to me," she said as she scratched her loveable dog behind the ears.

Her reverie was broken by the sound of her cell phone ringing. She looked at the name, smiled, and turned down the music volume.

"Hi, Josh. What's going on?"

ACKNOWLEDGMENTS

Once again, thanks go to Sandra Haven, Editor Extraordinaire, for finding the holes and recommending changes that improve the story.

Hats off to Kathleen Costello for doing the professional copyediting. Her grammar and punctuation are far superior to mine.

And a huge THANK YOU to my little sister Carleen aka "Carly" for playing my sidekick. Julia is much better with you at her side.

Finally I must thank my husband Steve for his patience and being my number one fan and supporter. I love you!

ABOUT THE AUTHOR

PJ Peterson is an author of mysteries that include a bit of medical intrigue surrounded by snippets of real life. A retired internist, she has transferred her curiosity of medical diagnostics to the challenge of creating books that satisfy the desire to solve mysteries.

If you enjoyed reading this fourth Julia Fairchild mystery, she would greatly appreciate your sharing a review (on Amazon) for other readers.

Thank you!

ALSO BY PJ PETERSON

Blind Fish Don't Talk

Rembrandt Rides a Bike

Pickled PInk in Paris

All available in e-book and paperback.